I0632232

# Bones in the Bayou

WREN AND RASCAL COZY MYSTERY, BOOK 5

## JUDITH A. BARRETT

WOBBLY CREEK, LLC

Bones in the Bayou

Wren and Rascal Cozy Mystery, Book 5

Published in the United States of America by Wobbly Creek, LLC

2024 Georgia

wobblycreek.com

Bones in the Bayou

Copyright ©2024 by Judith A. Barrett

All Rights Reserved. No parts of this book may be reproduced, stored, or transmitted in any form or by any means, electronic, mechanical, photocopying, recording, or otherwise, without the prior written permission of the copyright owner, except for brief excerpts for reviews.

Bones in the Bayou is a work of fiction. Names, characters, businesses, places, events, locales, and incidents either are the products of the author's imagination or used in a fictitious manner. Any resemblance to actual persons, living or dead, or actual events is purely coincidental.

Cover by Wobbly Creek, LLC

ISBN 978-1-953870-61-2 eBook

ISBN 978-1-953870-62-9 paperback

# Dedication

Bones in the Bayou is dedicated to the colors green and blue and to storytellers everywhere.

# Previously...

WREN

My name is Wren Weaver; I'm a freelance journalist and a camping enthusiast, so I was excited about the offer from a travel magazine publisher that combined my two passions. My original assignment was to write about four haunted campgrounds across the United States and to provide feedback on the trailers we used for camping.

Rascal, my four-year-old black and tan Labrador Retriever, with a smidgeon of Husky, went with me to our first haunted campground in Hidden Gulch, Arizona, where I met the cute and infuriating county marshal.

Even though we were in Hidden Gulch only a week, Marshal Justin Lewis and I became more than friends, and our relationship kept growing stronger as Rascal and I continued to our second, third, and finally, fourth assignment in Sirens Beach, Florida.

The Lost Pirate Campground became a record-breaker for me. I suffered a record number of injuries from falls, and when a severe storm smashed my camper van against a building, it was the second camper I had that was destroyed in less than a week.

It wasn't all bad, though, because I made two new friends, actually three counting my friend the ghostly pirate Captain X, broke up a smuggling ring, and stopped a killer.

It's not quite the end of the story; Justin surprised me by bringing my truck that had been in the repair shop in Mobile, Alabama, with our dream fifth wheel behind it to the Lost Pirate Campground. We'll be camping in pure luxury because I finally have a camper with running water and a toilet that can be flushed.

I must be getting soft, though, because after I swore the Lost Pirate Campground was my final article for the travel magazine, the publisher talked me into writing one more article about one more haunted campground. Justin, Rascal, and I are on our way to Louisiana.

JUSTIN

My name is Justin Lewis, and I'm the marshal at Hidden Gulch, Arizona; I moved to Hidden Gulch three years ago and discovered the slow pace of a small town was exactly what I needed to heal after I lost my wife in a car crash.

The single life suited me, and I was convinced I was immune to women until I met Wren. When she gazed at me with her emerald green eyes and spoke to me in her soft, Georgia accent, she melted my heart that I thought had frozen long ago. She's petite and looks fragile, but that green-eyed beauty with light brown hair and its streaks of red that look like fire is absolutely fearless, and she terrifies me with the chances she takes.

She promised the Forgotten Oasis Campground ghost, Thomas, that she'd be back in six weeks, and it's been a month since she left, which was far too long as far as I was concerned.

I couldn't stand to be away from her one more day, so I surprised her when she completed her fourth, and we thought last, article for the travel magazine. I flew to Mobile, Alabama, and picked up her truck and a new fifth wheel trailer, our dream camper that we had talked about.

We're on our way to Louisiana to another haunted campground. I don't care where we go as long as I'm with Wren and Rascal.

# Chapter One

The sound of gurgling woke Wren; she leaped out of bed, dashed toward the door, and crashed into the kitchen island; she fell with her arms flailing as she tried to maintain her balance. When she landed on her outflung left hand, she moaned and held her wrist.

"Are you okay?" Justin asked.

"No," Wren growled. "I forgot we were together in the fifth wheel trailer; I thought I was still alone with Rascal in the van, and someone was drowning right outside the door."

"You must have heard the coffee pot." Justin helped Wren to her feet, guided her to the dining table, and put a cup of coffee on the table in front of her. "How did you sleep?"

"Because the campground is close to the highway, I expected the rumble of traffic to keep me from getting a good night's sleep. I tried to stay awake to listen for it, but the sofa was comfortable, and I must have felt safe because you were here; I don't even remember falling asleep." Wren sipped her coffee. "Oof, it's hot. How long have you been awake?"

"Not long; what do you want for breakfast? Do you need ice for your wrist?"

"Just coffee, no ice," Wren grumbled then exhaled. "I'm not always this crabby in the morning."

Rascal yipped.

Wren glared at Rascal.

Justin kissed Wren's pouty mouth. "Rascal and I will go for a walk; relax with your coffee."

After they left, Wren exhaled. *I can take a shower without getting chilled from rushing back from the campground restroom.* Wren stripped and stepped into the trailer shower; after a soothing wash with her scrubbie and foaming shower wash followed by a relaxing shampoo, she rinsed in the hot water, then dressed and returned to her tepid coffee.

When Justin and Rascal came inside, Wren smiled. "Good morning."

"You smell good." Justin beamed as he fed Rascal. "How about one of my famous breakfast tacos?"

"If you're cooking breakfast, I'll wash dishes."

While Justin scrambled eggs and heated tortillas, Wren folded her bed linens, transformed her bed into the sofa, and replaced the cushions before she straightened the bathroom.

She peeked around the bathroom corner and into the bedroom. *Justin made the bed; I wonder if that's what he always does.*

Wren inhaled the heady aroma of the tortillas Justin warmed on a skillet; she stepped down the three steps to the main level. "I didn't know you cooked; breakfast smells wonderful."

"Thanks; I have only a few specialties, but I rarely cook when it's only me." Justin set their plates with the breakfast tacos on the table. "What do you know about the Cypress Knees Campground?"

After Wren pulled out her chair and sat, Rascal flopped down next to her. "The campground has only thirty sites, its sites are level, the restrooms are clean, and it's near the water. The online ratings and reviews are excellent."

"Nothing about the campground being haunted?" Justin refilled their coffee then joined Wren at the table.

"The website has a creepy vibe that hints of voodoo, and a few of the reviews mentioned it was haunted, but they rated it with five stars, so I guess that was a plus; one reviewer said the wailing disturbed her sleep, but she probably meant the wailing wind."

Justin picked up his taco, but before he took a bite, he asked, "What about Mahoneville? Did you research the town?"

"Are you kidding? Of course, I did; do you want to hear?" Wren smiled.

Justin nodded as he took a big bite.

"It was established by the New Brunswick French Acadians when the British forcibly deported them from Mahone Bay in the late 1700s; it's surrounded by swamp land, so the Cajun language and culture have been relatively untainted by any outside influence."

Justin returned her smile. "So, we'll be deep in the heart of Louisiana Cajun country. I speak Spanish, but I don't know any Cajun French or even French. What about you?"

"I spent a little time with a Cajun chef in Nebraska for a culinary magazine article, so I know a few cuss words and some particularly effective curses."

Justin's eyes twinkled. "Might come in handy."

When they finished eating, Wren washed and rinsed the dishes, and Justin dried them. While Justin put away the dishes and stowed the coffee maker, Wren secured the rest of the loose items.

After everything was in place, Wren buried her face in Justin's chest as she hugged him. After she raised her head to gaze into his eyes, he smiled as he leaned close and brushed away the hair that had fallen over her left eye Wren pulled him even closer for a sweet kiss that he shifted to a longing so intense that it took away her breath.

When Justin reluctantly released her, he smiled as he gently stroked her cheek. "Teamwork is a beautiful thing; bring in the slide outs, sweetie, and I'll disconnect the utilities, so we can hit the road."

After Justin entered the ramp for the interstate and headed west, Wren looked up from her phone. "I found an article that might be related to the haunted campground. In the early 1900s, a voodoo priestess who was the daughter of former slaves lived on the edge of a swamp west of New Orleans. Julia Brown was very influential in the community because of her charms and curses. She sat on her porch while she played her guitar and sang eerie songs; the scoffers in town ridiculed the disturbing words of one particular song, 'One day I'm going to die and take the whole town with me.' On the day of her funeral, September 29, 1915, a monstrous hurricane from the Gulf slammed into the coast of

Louisiana and wiped out entire towns, and the people perished in the terrible winds and rapidly rising water."

As they continued on the interstate, Wren stared at their surroundings. "It's so flat, and there's water on both sides of the road; it seems like we're traveling from one bridge to the next." Wren inhaled. "Even with the windows closed, I can smell and feel the dampness of the swamp."

Justin pointed at the water on Wren's side of the road. "Watch the pelican; he's cruising low for a snack."

Wren looked at Justin to see which direction he was pointing then peered out her side window.

"There he goes," Wren said as the pelican scooped up fish and swerved upward. "I almost missed seeing him; pelicans are much larger than I expected."

"They almost look too heavy to fly, don't they? We have a town coming up soon," Justin said. "Are you about ready to swoop in for some lunch?"

Rascal moaned from the back seat; Wren rolled her eyes.

Justin grinned. "Stick with me, Rascal; I got a million of them groaners."

Justin took the interstate exit ramp; when they reached the town limits, he said, "Help me look for pickup trucks."

"Up ahead on your side; a couple of men are walking across the road to my side where a bunch of pickups are parked; they're carrying white takeout sacks," Wren said.

Justin slowed then passed the parked trucks at a crawl. "Yep; sign says, 'Cajun Cooking', and the building's not much bigger than a shed. This is exactly what I hoped we'd find."

He parked in the empty lot next to where the pickups were. "Do you want to get out and stretch a little while I grab us some lunch, or would you rather go with me, or wait in the truck?"

"Rascal and I will get out, but we'll wait for you here."

While Justin was gone, and Rascal explored the empty lot, Wren's phone rang. Wren smiled and immediately answered.

"I'm not supposed to be calling you yet," Betsy whispered. "Are you alone?"

"Yes, Rascal's exploring a parking lot, and..."

Betsy interrupted Wren. "I'm not supposed to talk to you until Socorro gives me the all-clear, but she went into town, and Butch is working on one of his projects. Socorro told me I was sworn to secrecy, but that was strange because I didn't even know what the secret was. I have to tell you the latest, though. Remember our new teacher and Natalie at the diner? He finally proposed; Natalie's ring is beautiful, but they haven't set a date. I called it, didn't I? No one except you and a couple of other people at the grocery store know I suspected something was up when I saw Aaron and Justin in Tucson at the jewelry store. Isn't it great the mystery is solved? Oops, I have to go; Butch is coming into the office."

Betsy hung up.

Wren furrowed her brow. *I wonder if the secret was that Justin was on his way to Mobile. Betsy didn't know, or she would have told me, so that must be it.*

Justin returned with two white takeout sacks and a small brown one. "Anything happen while I was gone?"

"Betsy called, but that's all; why?"

Justin raised his eyebrows. "Because you are you, honey; things seem to just happen. Let's eat lunch in the trailer."

Justin opened the door then lowered the steps.

"Is it okay if I put out the dining table slide out?" Wren asked.

"Go ahead; we've got plenty of room, and we won't be here long."

After Wren slid out the dining area, Justin set the sacks on the table. "We have sweet tea, gumbo, and potato salad, which I understand is a normal side dish with gumbo, and for dessert, we have Louisiana swamp cake. When I saw how enormous the portions were, I ordered three meals and two pieces of cake, so we could have leftovers this evening."

Wren tasted her gumbo then took a bite of potato salad. "The gumbo is delicious; I was a little dubious about how the potato salad would go with gumbo, but the creaminess smooths out the spicy, doesn't it?"

Justin's mouth was full; he nodded.

After she ate half of her gumbo and potato salad, Wren wrapped her leftovers and put them into the refrigerator along with the third meal.

Wren examined the pieces of sheet cake covered with a thick chocolate frosting that dripped over the edges. "This looks gooey; I won't be able to eat more than half."

"Let's split one." Justin pulled out two small paper plates; after he cut a piece in half and scooped their cake and extra frosting onto their plates, Wren took a small bite of hers while Justin took a huge bite.

"Wow; chocolate cake with shredded coconut and pecans; is that marshmallow cream under the frosting? This is definitely chocolate heaven." Wren took another bite.

After he swallowed his first bite, Justin put down his fork. "I hope this freezes well, because it's too sweet for me."

Wren stared. "You don't like chocolate cake?"

Justin shuddered. "I love chocolate cake, but marshmallow cream has never been my favorite, and it's too melted into the cake to scrape it out." He carefully sliced away one corner of his cake, then cut it into four small bites. "These are mine for this week. The rest of the cake is yours."

Wren narrowed her eyes. "Are you sure you're not trying to be nice?"

"I'm positive."

Wren cut the two larger pieces of cake in half. "There, both of us have dessert for four days."

While Wren put all the pieces of cake, including Justin's small bites into a container, then put them into the freezer, Justin wiped down the dining table and gathered the trash.

As they returned to the interstate and continued west, Wren said, "After the cake is frozen, it will be easy to slice away the marshmallow cream, so you can have chocolate cake, as long as chocolate cake with pecans and coconut but no frosting is acceptable."

Justin glanced at Wren. "That's a brilliant idea, but you'd be giving up your cake."

Wren smiled. "I'll have your small bites, my half of each piece of cake, plus your marshmallow crème with frosting, so I'll be coming out ahead."

"It's the dessert math sharing formula, isn't it? Subtract what you don't want, add what you do want, and keep the small bites." Justin chuckled. "I'll have to remember that the next time I have a problem."

An hour later, Justin slowed for their exit. "Only forty-five minutes or so, depending on the road."

Justin maintained a slow, steady speed on the narrow two-lane road that had no shoulders. Wren flinched at every dip and sway; the back of her neck and her hands were clammy. She swallowed hard as she peered at Justin and smiled. *He is so cute.* He glanced at her and returned her smile.

*When I look at him, all my fears melt.* She turned to look at Rascal, who was sleeping in the back seat. *Rascal is relaxed.* She exhaled. *I'm used to driving and being in control; Justin is in control: I can chill.*

Wren leaned back and closed her eyes. The dips and sways rocked her to sleep.

Wren woke with a start when the truck slowed. "Sweetheart, we're here."

When Wren sat up, she saw the massive wooden welcoming sign with easily read, carved letters that had been painted with bright, white paint: "Bienvenue en Cypress Knees Campground."

The wide driveway was covered with gravel that crunched under their tires. The well-maintained office building at the end of the driveway mimicked the style of a wooden shanty on the edge of a river or swamp except for the camellias and irises that were growing along the front of the building. A six-foot tall alligator that had been carved from a tree stood on the shanty porch; its right paw was raised in greeting.

The campsite pads were concrete with recently mowed grass next to each pad; a little over half of the campsites were occupied.

"This is beautiful," Wren said. "None of the other campgrounds were as inviting as this one."

Justin pointed. "The last row of five campsites must be permanent residents; their sites are certainly well-decorated with flowers, garden flags, and plants. They must have a nightly gathering. Did you notice the chairs around a fire ring at the far end of their row?"

Wren sat forward to see the end of the row. "It's definitely set up for an evening get-together."

As they strolled to the office, Wren said, "The pool is gorgeous; the building next to it must be the restrooms and laundry."

Justin added, "I can smell the swamp, but it isn't unpleasant, is it?"

"Not at all; it adds to the atmosphere." Wren tilted her head as she examined the porch at the registration office. "Wonder why there's a mirror outside the building next to the door and a tiny box with marbles in it."

"Did you notice the dog park? It's fenced and grassed," Justin said.

When the three of them went inside the office, a young woman with creamy brown skin, deep brown eyes, and black hair who wore a camo-brown shirt with a nametag that said Babette met them at the registration counter. When she smiled, her eyes twinkled. "*Bienvenue*, Welcome. Are you da Lewis party of two?" Her soft voice had the lilt and the cadence of the Louisiana Cajun dialect.

"No," Wren said.

"Yes," Justin said.

Wren gaped at Justin.

Babette's laugh was musical. "Y'all are fun. I have a reservation for Wren Weaver and Justin Lewis. The CEO of our new franchise called me and gave me a heads up. You two are VIPs, as far as he's concerned, so you're my VIPs too."

Babette opened a drawer. "Sit, Rascal."

Rascal immediately dropped into a sit, and Babette gave him a treat. "Good boy."

She rubbed his ears, and Rascal moaned. Babette cooed, "He tole me all about you, too, Rascal, and what a good boy you are; you're a VIP too."

She circled their site with a permanent felt-tip marker and drew a line from the registration office to their site. "There's a group that gets together at the end of the row next to yours every night for songs and swappin' stories. You'll hear 'em, but don't you worry 'bout them keeping you up. They all leave for their jobs early in the morning. They slip out all silent-like before dawn; you'd think they were ghosts."

"Thanks." Justin picked up the map, and the three of them headed toward the door.

Before Justin opened the door, Babette continued, "I forgot to mention we have a well-marked walking trail that is a little over a mile long. If you'd like to jog or maybe take Rascal for an off-leash walk or run, it's a great way to start your morning. Speaking of early, if you're interested in seeing how alligator traps are set, let me know; my brother's partner won't be back from Texas until later tomorrow, and Armand wouldn't mind having some company when he goes to set them out in the morning before it gets too muggy."

Justin glanced at Wren who grinned.

"We'd love it," he said.

"That's great; he wanted me to go with him, but I couldn't find nobody to fill in at the campground on such short notice, so I was going to have to post a closed for the morning sign. Papa always taught us it's not safe to be on the water alone. Be here at six; have your coffee but don't eat nothin' because Armand will take you to his favorite diner up the bayou and buy you breakfast. Rascal, you won't like it much because the boat's kind of small for four; you're welcome to keep me company."

Rascal yipped; the three of them climbed into the truck and headed toward their campsite.

After Justin and Wren unhitched the truck and leveled the fifth wheel, Justin connected the utilities with Rascal's supervision while Wren carried her computer bag inside and put out the slides.

When Justin and Rascal came inside, Wren had the coffee set up for the next morning and was setting up her computer.

"If you want time to write, Rascal and I can go exploring," Justin said.

"I want to go exploring too." Wren peered at him over her computer screen.

"Okay, we'll sit at the picnic table to give you some concentration time; I'll call Pat to see if there's anything that needs my attention at the office."

"Pat's been a senior deputy for a long time; won't he think you don't trust his judgment?"

"Not at all; I'll tell him Rascal and I are trying to stay out of your way, and he's our excuse." Justin's mouth twitched in his effort to hide his smile.

Wren giggled. "As long as it's all my fault, it's fine."

Wren found the article on Aunt Julia Brown and jotted down notes before she summarized the story. Her phone buzzed a text from Crystal at the Lost Pirate Campground.

"Call when you have time."

Wren called Crystal.

"Hey, Wren. I've had two strange phone calls today. The first one was a man who said he was your brother. Your ex-friend doesn't have much imagination, does he? He wanted to know if you were still here. I told him you weren't because some guy was stalking you, and you went to his folks' house on the advice of the FBI. He hung up on me. It would have been laughable except I'm worried your ex-friend is starting to obsess over you."

Wren frowned. "You might be right; I'm not sure what else I can do about Blake."

"Stay close to Justin and keep your powder dry," Crystal said.

"Got it."

"The second call was a woman who said she was your sister. Wren, I wouldn't have doubted her for a second if it hadn't been for Blake. She wanted to know if you were still here, and get this...was there a man with you."

"What?"

"Threw me too. I told her I was sorry that she missed you because you had already left to go to your parents' house for your brother's birthday, and there was not a man with you. Wren, do you have a sister that I need to apologize to?"

"No, I'm an only child; at least, that's what Mom told me. What a strange call."

"My only explanation is that Blake talked someone into calling," Crystal said.

"He's pretty persuasive, so you're probably right."

"How's everything? I need details."

"Justin is dreamy, and the fifth wheel is glorious; for your personal logistics information, I'm sleeping on the sofa," Wren said.

"I know you're being sensible and not rushing into things, but I'm so sorry to hear that." Crystal chuckled as she hung up.

# Chapter Two

Wren rolled her eyes and turned back to her laptop. She found five more recent articles that were duplicates of the first. She scrunched her face and snorted. *Blatant plagiarism: these newer articles copied the original almost word for word but didn't bother to mention their source.*

Her phone buzzed a text from Kendra, her editor. "Where are you?"

*I need to update Kendra with my news.* Wren replied, "Louisiana. I'll call later."

Before she sent it, Wren peeked out the window at Justin, who was still on his phone and pacing. *He's deep in thought. I'll call Kendra instead.*

When Kendra answered, Wren said, "I'm in Louisiana..."

Wren continued with telling her about Justin surprising her, the fifth wheel, the legend of Julia Brown, and the Louisiana campground.

"That is so romantic of Justin; I'm impressed," Kendra said. "Just when I think there couldn't possibly be another haunted campground, Charlie and the CEO manage to come up with one, although from what you've said, it sounds like it was a good business decision for the CEO to bring them into his franchise. So, when am I going to get a draft to review?"

"I'll send you the link to the article about Julia Brown. I'm hoping you'll have a draft by Friday; it seems like it should be very simple to write, but I haven't had one article that was simple or followed a local legend, have I?" Wren sighed.

"What about your blog? It's about time for another one."

"Thanks for the reminder; we're going for a boat ride on the bayou tomorrow morning."

"That's wonderful; you'll be getting some local color, which will be a great introduction for your campground travel article. What's Justin doing?"

"He and Rascal went outside, so I'd have a little quiet time to write. We're going to explore the campground."

"You had better go; I'll watch for your blog post."

After they hung up, Wren sent the link to the original Julia Brown article to Kendra then opened the fifth wheel door.

Justin stopped pacing. "Wren's ready to go exploring; thanks for the update." He hung up and smiled. "Shall we start with the dog park?" Justin picked up Rascal's leash from the picnic table and shoved it into his back pocket.

Rascal trotted alongside Wren as Justin put his arm around Wren's shoulder. When they reached the dog park, Justin opened the gate, and Rascal raced around the perimeter four times before he darted back to Wren and Justin who had sat on the bench.

"I think it's a great dog park too," Wren said.

Rascal grinned then began his intense investigation of the smells lingering along the fence and in the grass.

"What did Pat have to say?" Wren asked.

Justin frowned as he gazed at his feet. "Nothing much; just office stuff."

Wren glared at him. "Excuse me? Have you forgotten who you are talking to? What's wrong?"

Justin snorted. "That's not fair; I was weakened by sitting too close to you." He lightly brushed her jawline with his fingertips. "Your skin is so soft, and I keep watching your mouth because I want to kiss it."

"Ah." Wren kissed him. "So, what's wrong?"

Justin exhaled. "Your interrogation techniques are amazingly effective. Our newest deputy, Jake, quit, and Pat feels guilty."

"Pat? Why does he feel guilty?"

"She asked him where I was, and he told her it was none of her business."

Wren laughed. "Sorry, but is it okay if I love Pat's style? Why was she asking about you?"

"She told Pat she had broken off the engagement with our new pharmacist, and she needed to talk to me because I understood her."

Wren snorted. "Bless her heart."

Justin side-glanced Wren. "Did you just give her a Georgia bless her heart?"

Wren fluttered her eyelashes. "Sho 'nuf, darlin'."

Justin laughed. "You are such a trip."

When he stopped laughing, he rose from the bench. "Let's walk around the campground and see what everybody else has."

When they rounded the second row, Justin said, "Pat invited the new pharmacist to lunch and found out..."

Wren interrupted, "that the pharmacist broke off the engagement."

Justin smirked. "I can't tell you how happy I am that you are finally wrong. No, they were never engaged; the new pharmacist's real fiancée will be in Hidden Gulch next week to visit and look for a house."

Wren stopped. "What?"

"The pharmacist's fiancée is a tax lawyer for a large corporation and works remotely, so she can live anywhere. The wedding is scheduled to be held in two months at her parents' home church in Tucson. Pat was certain Jake had a phony, heartbreaking song and dance prepared for my benefit. He said when she started crying and said he was hateful and didn't understand, he said maybe she should talk it out with another woman..."

Wren interrupted. "Did she make a sarcastic remark and mention me?"

"How did you know?"

Wren told him about Crystal's call. "I'm positive Jake was trying to find you. You might want to tell Pat to document everything. I know I'm being paranoid, but there's a possibility she's unhinged enough to sue Pat to manipulate you. I know you don't care much for Cody, but he's a talented lawyer; maybe Pat should get in touch with him."

Justin nodded. "If Jake decides to play dirty, Cody is definitely the right lawyer to be in Pat's corner. Cody understands the dark side, doesn't he?"

"You have a terrible attitude when it comes to Cody, did you know that? He'll go all out for Pat; you can't deny that Cody loves a good fight as long as it isn't his."

"I suppose; maybe I should call Pat now."

"I think so; why don't you sit at our picnic table while Rascal and I wander around? Maybe Rascal and I will see what Babette has in the store that we absolutely have to have."

"That will work. I won't be long."

Wren stopped at their trailer for some cash before she and Rascal headed to the registration building. When they went inside, Babette was on the phone and doodling while she listened. She glanced at Wren and wiggled her fingers in greeting. Rascal trotted to her, and she put down her pen long enough to give Rascal a treat.

Wren browsed the items on the local crafts shelf with feigned interest when Babette tapped her pen and resumed doodling then whispered, "Honey, you gotta do what's best for your family. I get that."

Wren examined the different styles of salt and pepper shakers and smiled at the dark green avocado set. The pepper half of the avocado had the familiar brown seed embedded in the creamy green, and the salt half was curved where the seed fit, so the set was flush when put together.

Babette continued, "I don't like being threatened either, but family comes first, doesn't it?"

Babette frowned and shook her head. "What? That much? I'll help you as much as I can; I'll get a night job at the poultry plant."

A tear slipped down Babette's face. "No, it's fine; it's what friends do, and I want to help you."

After she hung up, Babette rubbed away the tears from her cheek and flipped over the sack she'd been writing on then added it to the small stack next to the register. Babette sighed then glanced toward Wren who had quickly shifted her attention to the avocado saltshaker in her hand.

Wren put the saltshaker back on the shelf before she met Babette's gaze and smiled. "This is a really cute set, and I love how compact it is; it belongs in a camper, doesn't it?"

"It's been a popular item; that's the last one we have left." Babette returned Wren's smile. "Shall I set it aside for you while you think about it?"

"I'd like that."

Wren took the salt and pepper shakers to the desk; Babette carefully wrapped the set in tissue paper. Wren smiled as she pulled out the cash she had stuck into her pocket. "I thought about it; the set is perfect for our camper."

"Oh, good; it's definitely you." Babette rang up the sale and gave Wren her change. While she put the set in a small bag, Babette asked, "Do you have any salt and pepper?"

Wren frowned. "I don't remember seeing any; I need to start a list of what we need to get the next time we go into town."

"We can't have that." Babette hurried to the last aisle then returned with a cardboard set of disposable salt and pepper shakers and dropped them into the sack. "Here you go."

When Wren reached for her pocket, Babette said, "Don't bother; you're doing me a favor because they were taking up space on the shelf. Did I tell you to sit outside a spell this evening? When our permanent folks come home from work, it's a long-standing tradition for those that are here to wave and welcome them home; it will most likely get you an invite to the firepit party. You'll hear some tall tales that might help you with your article."

"Thank you; we'll do that."

Before Wren and Rascal reached the door, Babette said, "I thought about opening the store a little later in the mornings, but not tomorrow because Rascal and I have a date. I will put a note on the door about the change of hours so everyone will know in advance."

When they neared the trailer, Justin waved.

Wren smiled and returned his wave. "Justin's still pacing, but he's been watching for us, Rascal."

Before they reached the trailer, Justin hung up and stuck his phone in his back pocket then strode to join them.

He put his arm around Wren and kissed her lightly. "I missed you. What did you find at the store?"

"A set of salt and pepper shakers. I'll show you when we go inside. What did Pat say?"

"He liked the idea of calling Cody; he said to tell you thanks for suggesting it because he knew I wouldn't have suspected anything underhanded in Jake's motives and certainly wouldn't have thought of Cody."

Wren nodded. "Betsy told me her dad always said, 'Trust but verify', and it really stuck with me."

Justin stopped as he reached for the trailer door and squinted at Wren. "Betsy?"

"I was as surprised as you are; sometimes it seems like Betsy is really random, then she comes up with a spark that is pure genius."

"Trust and verify," Justin mumbled.

When they were inside, Wren pulled out the avocado salt and pepper shaker, unwrapped it, and placed it and the disposable set on the dining table.

"What do you think?" Wren separated them.

Justin smiled. "Perfect match for our Arizona camper; our avocado will fit in the top drawer where we have the paper plates and napkins."

"Babette gave me the salt and pepper, so we could fill the avocado set."

Justin pulled out his pocketknife, pried open the lid from the pepper, and frowned. "I might make a mess."

Wren pulled out a small paper plate and put it on the table. "If you pour into the avocado pepper over the plate, you can catch any overflow."

While Justin carefully poured the pepper into the avocado pepper container, Wren folded the paper sack, then placed it in an empty cabinet over the recliners. "Babette told me when the workers come home in the evening, it's traditional to sit outside and wave, and we might be invited to the firepit."

"We can do that; does that make us locals?" Justin pried off the lid of the disposable saltshaker.

"Maybe not completely outsiders."

After the salt and pepper shakers were filled, Justin said, "Since there is no way for me to be on duty, and we don't need to go anywhere, I bought a bottle of wine in Mobile. Would you like a glass before or after dinner?"

"What a great surprise. After dinner, then we can listen to the music and relax."

Justin furrowed his brow. "Am I cutting into your writing time?"

"Not at all; Kendra reminded me it was time to blog, but I'll blog tomorrow after our boat ride on the bayou."

Rascal whined.

"I'll bet Rascal heard a truck. Ready to be neighborly?" Justin asked.

Rascal investigated their campsite while Wren sat at the picnic table, and Justin examined the tires on the truck and the fifth wheel.

"Is everything okay?" Wren asked when he joined her.

"It's been on my mind, and it was something to do instead of pacing. I might go into town tomorrow afternoon while you're writing and get a few tools. I need a tire gauge, and it might be smart to have an air compressor just in case."

When a truck traveled down the driveway then passed them, Wren waved, and Justin nodded. The driver returned Justin's nod.

After the first truck, a parade of trucks rolled in.

"Twelve," she said when the last truck beeped at their wave and nod.

"You were counting?" Justin asked.

Wren tilted her head. "I guess so; I didn't realize it."

While Wren peered at the driveway to watch for trucks, Justin stood behind her and massaged her shoulders. "I thought with all your falls, your neck and shoulders might be a little sore; your muscles are tight."

Wren exhaled. "That feels fantastic; I didn't even realize how achy I was."

Justin sat next to her and put his arm around her while she leaned on his chest. "Mmm; this is nice," she whispered.

Rascal whined as a wizened woman leaned on a twisted cypress stick as she limped toward them. "Mind if I join you for a spell?"

"Please do," Wren said.

Justin jumped up and offered his arm to the woman then assisted her as she sat across from Wren.

Rascal nudged the old woman's elbow, and she chuckled as she rubbed his ears; her voice had the same soft lilt and accent as Babette. "You two must be honeymooners; welcome to the Cypress Knees Campground; I'm Desirada."

"Nice to meet you," Wren and Justin said.

Justin continued, "This is Wren, and I'm Justin."

The old woman peered closely at Wren. "You remind me of another pretty girl." Desirada trembled. "Forgive me; I got lost in my old memories there for a minute. It's right nice to meet y'all too. We'd be honored if you'd join us at our campfire soiree this evening. Our little group can guarantee genuine Cajun music, tall tales, and laughs. We start round about dark; bring your camp chairs and whatever beverage you enjoy."

Desirada quickly rose. "See you later."

After she was gone, Wren said, "We should have corrected her about being honeymooners; it's going to be really awkward later."

"She didn't give us a chance, did she? She was like a dancing dust devil that flitted across the desert and threw a little dazzle dust over us then disappeared."

Wren stared at him. "Where did that come from? I'll have to write that down."

Justin chuckled as they went inside. "It must have been the dazzle dust."

Wren pulled out their leftovers from the refrigerator and smiled. "I'll cook tonight."

While Wren warmed their gumbo on the stovetop burner, Justin fed Rascal; Wren put the potato salad on the table along with small paper plates, forks, and spoons then pulled out two cold bottles of water from the refrigerator. When the gumbo was hot, Wren poured it into large paper bowls, with Justin's portion larger than hers.

While they were eating, Justin said, "I have a feeling our gumbo will set the mood for our evening; so, how are you going to tell Desirada that we aren't honeymooning?"

"Me? Why not you?"

"I asked you first."

"What if we skip trying to straighten it out?" Wren asked.

"Gumbo is a great leftover." Justin took another big bite.

Wren glared at him then scooped up gumbo with her spoon.

After they finished eating, Justin cleared the table while Wren pulled out their cake from the freezer. She carefully slipped a knife between the marshmallow cream and cake of both pieces then put the pieces of cake on one plate and the marshmallow cream and frosting on the other. She put the plate with Justin's cake and a clean fork at his place.

Justin hugged her and tilted up her chin to gaze into her eyes. "Is that a bribe?"

"Whatever works."

When she smiled, Justin leaned down and kissed her open mouth.

After he released her, she exhaled and fanned her face with her hand, Scarlett O'Hara style. "You're pretty hot in the bribe department yourself, Marshal."

He laughed and hugged her tight. "I love you, sweetheart."

"I love you so much; did you know your cake is thawing?" Wren mumbled into his chest.

"It should be, as steamy as it is in here. Sit down, I'll serve you." Justin stared at the two plates. "Wouldn't you like some cake with your frosting? I'll give you one of the cake pieces."

"Give me half of one; plop it on top of the frosting. I'll eat what I want; we'll toss the rest to avoid a sugar coma."

While they ate dessert, Justin said, "You know what would be absolutely perfect for this cake? Real whipped cream."

"I would have said ice cream," Wren said.

Justin finished his cake. "What about ice cream with whipped cream on top?"

Wren rolled her eyes. "We'd be back to sugar coma." She stared at her plate. "I can't eat the rest of the cake."

Justin stabbed her cake with his fork and popped it into his mouth.

Wren shook her head and rinsed their forks and spoons then left their silverware in the sink while Justin tossed the paper plates and bowls into the trash.

Rascal's ears perked up at the sound of a fiddle being tuned, and he whined.

"Are you ready for the soiree?" Justin asked.

"I have some natural bug repellent that we can spritz on our necks and arms, then I'm ready."

After Wren sprayed Justin and herself, she said, "All ready, but I'm not sure I'm interested in taking a glass of wine."

"I'll pour our wine into our travel mugs, so we won't be drowning bugs while we're enjoying the music."

Wren smiled. "That's brilliant; I was trying to figure out how I could sip my wine while I covered my glass with my hand."

Justin pulled out the camping chairs from a compartment while Wren carried their travel mugs, and Rascal dashed to the end of the row when the disorganized tuning pulled together into bouncy, Cajun music, and the volume of chatter increased in a vain attempt to shout over the music.

As they neared the group, Rascal joined them and whined as Desirada hobbled to greet them; Wren strained to hear Desirada's voice. "Come along; I'll introduce you to everyone, but you don't have to remember no names because I don't know half of them myself."

When they reached the fire pit, Desirada raised her hand, and a hush fell over the group.

"Everybody, this here's our people."

While the group welcomed them, the fiddle player strolled to Justin and whispered; Justin glanced toward Wren then nodded before he pulled out his phone, shrugged, and returned it to his pocket.

The fiddler returned to his spot and held up his hand. When everyone quieted down, he pointed to a large pot that sat on a tall, three-legged stool. His voice had the low timbre of a classical bass singer. "Just like we say every night, this here's our gumbo pot for those who are moved to toss in a tip, but it ain't a requirement as long as you are enjoying our tunes."

After the music resumed, Justin set up their chairs close to the musicians.

Wren tugged on Justin's shirtsleeve, and he leaned toward her.

"What was that?" she yelled to be heard over the accordion.

Justin leaned close and nibbled on her ear; Wren giggled.

"Tell you later," he whispered.

"A text from Mom," he shouted. "I'll call her later."

Wren smiled and held up a thumb; Justin returned her smile and put his arm around her. When he pulled her closer and squeezed, she giggled.

Rascal put his chin on her knee, and she scratched behind his ear. *Why do I feel like we're putting on a show for an audience who is watching every move and judging us?*

Wren leaned against Justin and sipped her wine while she tapped her toe. *Love the music.*

After forty-five minutes, the accordion player nodded his head, and the band finished up their tune.

His tenor voice was a melodious complement to the fiddler's bass. "Time for some yarns of the swamp."

An elderly woman who sat across the fire from Wren pulled her shawl from over her head to her shoulders. "Thank you, Remy. In honor of *nos amis*, our friends, this is the story of how the Cypress Knees Campground got its name." The group murmured in approval.

Wren glanced at Justin, and he winked. Wren smiled. *Babette set this up.*

"Long before Tante Julia Brown was born, cypress trees was plentiful in the swamp." The elderly woman's sing-song voice was reminiscent of the whistling wind in a storm.

"Their roots was shallow, though; when da hurricanes hit, pine trees on the solid land weren't uprooted because their tap roots held them fast, and they lived, even though their tops were sheared. The cypress trees with their weak roots that were close to the surface fell over like a house of cards and drowned in the swamp. All the folk mourned the loss of the trees and said cypress would soon be no more."

Wren's eyes widened as an emaciated young girl with coal-black skin appeared next to the old woman. The young girl, who wore a tattered, shapeless dress made from a flour sack, met Wren's gaze; after the waif glanced at the old woman, she shook her head then waved to Wren before she disappeared.

Wren reflexively raised her hand, then quickly lowered it as she glanced at Justin, who was focused on the storyteller. Wren scanned the rest of the crowd; all of them were listening intently to the storyteller except Desirada, who raised her eyebrows at Wren and nodded.

Wren leaned back and turned her attention to the storyteller. *Desirada knows I saw the little girl.*

The woman continued her story. "On the day Julia Brown was born, the midwife called for the healer because the baby had a bleeding open wound in the shape of a cross on her chest over her heart. The healer proclaimed the baby was a protector, and the baby's heart would always bleed for her people. Julia Brown's mama was in so much distress over the pain her daughter would bear that the healer applied an oil, and the open wound closed; it was a miracle, and a sign of what lay ahead for Julia Brown."

"A miracle or a warning?" a woman muttered.

The storyteller raised her voice. "Penelope, it was a protection for the protector because nobody ever knew of her wound except for her mama, the midwife, and the healer."

"And Tante Julia Brown; don't forget that, Simone," Penelope said.

Simone nodded. "Even when she was a toddler, Julia Brown knew she was also a healer; she would pick up a fallen, dead bird and blow on it, then sing a joyful song when the bird fluttered its wings and flew away. When she was five, she played her uncle's guitar and sang mournful tunes that made grown men weep for all those who had been lost to cholera and the yellow fever."

"She had a dark side too," Penelope said.

Simone scowled. "We don't talk about that."

The two women glared at each other while everyone else around the fire held their breath.

When the second woman flounced away from the group, the storyteller said, "There was no dark side to that woman of light."

A man said, "Julia Brown carried the curse of her wound that bled inside her chest, and even after four different husbands and many men, she never bore a child until..."

Simone interrupted him. "That's not true; she was always faithful to her man."

"She was a woman of passion," the man said.

"Who's telling this story? Me or you?" the storyteller growled.

The man put up his hands. "Your story, Simone."

"Thought so," the storyteller muttered before she continued, "The cypress knees reappeared after Tante Julia Brown stood near the edge of the swamp and cursed the hurricane and forbid it to touch her swamp as long as she lived; she commanded the cypress trees to rise up in defiance of the soulless killer winds and water."

The man added, "The child she wanted so badly came because Tante Julia Brown swore she'd give her child to the hurricane in exchange for the cypress trees, and the knees appeared to anchor the cypress."

"And the child, who was named Mara, wept bitter tears when her mama died; when the hurricane came to claim Mara, the knees banded together and kept Mara in the swamp, and the enraged hurricane decimated the land and all its people," Simone said.

The man nodded. "Julia Brown knew that's what the hurricane would do, but she didn't warn the people because the hurricane would hear and would defeat the knees. Julia Brown sacrificed the people to keep her daughter out of the grasp of the hurricane."

"That's absolutely not true. That's not the spirit of Julia Brown, and anyone who lays claim to the black arts and Julia Brown is a liar and a cheat and will be exposed. Mara guards the people now." Simone rose and spit into the fire before she flipped her shawl over her head and left.

Al and Remy exchanged glances, then the fiddler tapped his toe and called out in his deep voice, "One, two…"

The music resumed with a classic two-step, and three couples jumped up to dance. Wren laughed and clapped at their agility; Justin checked his phone then stepped away from the fire and into the dark.

After four more dance tunes, Remy played a long, drawn-out chord; when he had everyone's attention, he said, "Me and Al will end the evening with a waltz, so grab your favorite dance partner and give 'er a squeeze."

The group cheered and whistled. While the talented dancers waltzed around the fire, Justin returned to his seat; after he put his arm around Wren, he kissed her cheek. "We'll talk when we get back to the trailer. Are you enjoying the music?"

Wren smiled. "It's been a wonderful evening."

When the song was over, everyone applauded and cheered while the band bowed then packed their instruments in their cases.

The fiddler strolled over to join Wren and Justin while Justin folded up their camping chairs.

"There are many versions of the story of Julia Brown, but nobody spins their yarn with more passion than our Simone." His eyes twinkled. "The woman who argued with her, Penelope, is her sister. Tonight was pretty mild; we've had to drag those two feisty, old women apart from time to time. The man was her nephew; he likes to goad her on, but he knows when to stop."

Rascal dashed to the trailer. As they strolled along behind him, Justin put his arm around Wren's shoulders, and she leaned her head against him.

"Was this our first actual date?" she asked.

Before he could reply, Wren continued, "Or did our coffee date with milkshakes count?"

Justin chuckled. "Absolutely not; we politely shook hands."

"True, and we followed it up with the impromptu lunch that wasn't really a date either."

"If I let you kiss me goodnight, this can be our first kissing date," Justin said.

Wren stopped and her mouth quivered as she tried to keep back a smile.

"Are you okay, honey?" Justin asked.

She wrapped her arms around his neck and pulled him close.

Justin kissed her gently then hugged her. "I expect a great goodnight kiss since we've already had our first kissing date."

When they reached the trailer, Wren asked, "Do you always make your bed?"

"Always, unless I get a call in the middle of the night; in that case, I'm wishfully hoping I can go back to bed before morning. What about you?"

Wren nodded. "I always do too. I had friends in school that never made their beds; their arguments were they were airing out their beds, and why make it anyway if it's going to be messed up again that night?"

"They're a lot hardier than I am; I'm too delicate to be sleeping on lumpy bed linens," Justin said. "Why did you ask?"

"I want to know everything about you, and by the way, I can think of a lot of ways to describe you, but delicate is not one I would have considered."

"Give me a list."

Wren giggled. "That reminded me of all the times you told me to send you a selfie."

"I need a photo of you; let's take a selfie together."

When they were inside the trailer, Justin asked, "How's your wine?"

"I still have most of it; I decided I'd enjoy it more when we're relaxing together in the trailer."

"So did I; we have some crackers and cheese. How about a party date?"

"Sounds nice."

After they were seated on the sofa, Justin put his arm around Wren, and she snuggled close to him.

"Selfie time." Wren patted the sofa next to her, and Rascal jumped up. She put her arm around him.

"Your phone or mine?" she asked.

"My arm is longer." Justin pulled out his phone.

Wren looked up at his phone and smiled. "Say cheese, Rascal."

Justin snapped several photos then they scrolled through them.

"Rascal has the best smile, don't you think?" Justin said.

"I like these two." Wren pointed.

"I do too; I'll send both of them to you."

While they sipped their wine and munched on crackers and cheese, Wren asked, "What do you want to talk about?"

"Nothing special."

Wren raised her eyebrows.

Justin shrugged. "The text was the local sheriff; he asked me to meet him at our trailer. We chatted a bit; he's come to a dead end on a long-running extortion case. All he has is rumors, but he wanted me to know in case I heard something. He said everybody already knows I'm a marshal in Arizona, but I'm not a threat to anyone because I'm so focused on you."

Wren snuggled closer. "Glad I can help."

Justin chuckled then put down his tumbler of wine and tilted up her chin to gaze at her face.

When Wren handed him her tumbler, he put it on the floor next to the plate of crackers and cheese, then he kissed her.

Wren leaned back when he released her and stroked his jawline with her fingertips. "We might be a little out of practice, but why don't I show you my version of a third date goodnight kiss."

After a long, soulful kiss, Wren sighed. "That was wonderful; it's getting late, and we have to get up early."

Justin buried his face in her neck. She scrunched her shoulder to protect her neck. "Your five o'clock shadow whiskers tickle."

"Too bad; do you plan to shower tonight or in the morning?" His voice was muffled as he lightly kissed her neck.

Wren sighed. "Tonight."

Justin sat up. "You first."

After her shower, Wren quickly dried then put on her pajamas. When she joined Justin in the living area, her eyes widened. "You didn't have to set up my bed."

"I wanted to; my turn for the shower; Rascal and I have already been outside, so you can climb into bed."

Wren snuggled down into the covers; she listened to the relaxing waterfall as Justin showered.

When he came to her bedside, he kissed her lightly. "Goodnight, sweetheart." Justin turned off the lights and sighed as he headed to his bedroom.

Wren mumbled, "I love you."

She closed her eyes and listened to the light wind that whispered, "Mara" as it rustled the leaves in the trees, and the trees groaned. Wren rolled over. *It's my overactive imagination.*

# Chapter Three

A loud click and the sound of a bubbling cauldron startled Wren. *What was that click?* Her heart raced while she struggled to get away before she was shot or was burned by the hot vat of boiling liquid that threatened to overflow into the fire, but the dark form that lingered near her bed had spun her into a cocoon.

She opened her eyes and exhaled in relief. *That's my recliner; I'm in the trailer.* Wren tried to sit up. *I'm all wrapped up in my sheet.*

After she untangled herself, she looked around. *It's the coffee maker; Justin and Rascal must have gone outside.*

Wren checked her phone and snorted. *My alarm goes off in three minutes.*

She turned off her alarm and stretched before she grabbed her clothes and dashed to the bathroom to dress. While Wren brushed her hair, she heard the click of the door as it opened.

"I poured your coffee earlier, so it would be cool enough for you." Justin closed the trailer door.

"Thank you; I wasn't awake enough to see it."

Rascal scrambled up the three steps to greet Wren. After she scratched Rascal's ears, Justin handed her the cup of coffee; she sat at the dining table and stared into her cup.

After Wren sipped her coffee, she said, "I've been having trouble with being completely disoriented when I wake up in the morning. I'm working the sound of the coffee maker into my nightmares, but it isn't the fault of the coffee maker."

Justin joined her at the table. "What is it?"

"It feels like foreboding to me, and if it had started this morning, I could blame the campground, but we were in the Mobile campground last night, and it was the farthest thing removed from being haunted."

"Could it be stress because I showed up? Am I putting too much pressure on you? It was a bad idea, wasn't it?"

Wren glared at Justin. "No, it wasn't; I'm perfectly capable of scaring myself without your help."

Justin examined her face; when his mouth twitched, he sipped his coffee. "Yes, dear."

Wren giggled. "Glad we got that out of the way; what's the weather like?"

"There's a mist over the swamp, and the humidity is so high that it feels soupy; it looks eerie, but I suspect it's normal for here."

"I'll put up my hair, so it won't stick to my neck."

While Wren pulled up her hair into a ponytail, Justin asked, "Do you want to take your coffee with you?"

"No, I'm looking forward to some good Cajun coffee with chicory this morning."

Wren put on her ball cap and a long-sleeved shirt over her T-shirt and shoved her light jacket into her backpack before they left.

On their way to the registration office, Justin asked, "How did you sleep?"

"Okay; what about you?"

"I had a little trouble getting to sleep; I must still be on Arizona time. You seemed a little restless while I was making coffee. I was afraid I was bothering you."

"Not at all; I woke up a minute or two before my alarm would have gone off."

When they went into the registration office, Babette's eyes were puffy and red.

"What's wrong?" Wren asked.

Babette's voice cracked. "Armand called; our Tante Simone died sometime in the night."

"I'm really sorry," Wren said.

"Thank you; Armand said she told her Julia Brown story last night; I'm glad you were there." Babette sniffled. "No one could tell a story like Tante Simone. Armand will be here in a few minutes." Babette rubbed Rascal's face. "I start my new job this afternoon; you'll still keep me company this morning, won't you, Rascal?"

Justin glanced at Wren and motioned toward the front door.

Wren nodded, and he stepped out to the porch.

Babette shook her head. "It's not right because Tante Simone went to the doctor for her checkup last week; the doc said Tante Simone would outlive us all. When I was a little girl, I stayed with Tante Simone after school until Mama got home from work. After I did my homework, Tante Simone would check it. If it was perfect, she would tell me stories."

Wren smiled. "It was perfect all the time, wasn't it?"

Babette returned her smile. "Always; I breezed through school because of the fanciful Cajun stories Tante Simone told me."

Justin opened the door. "Armand's here."

Babette patted Wren's hand. "Thanks for listening; Rascal and I will be fine."

As the three of them headed to the boat, Armand said, "Babette and Tante Simon were very close; how is she doing?"

"She's taking it hard, but she has wonderful memories, so that's a blessing," Wren said.

"A woman who has worked at the campground when Babette needed a fill-in will be at the campground later to help Babette; I know she's grateful that Rascal is with her this morning."

When they reached the flatbottom boat, Armand handed Wren and Justin life vests. "I had planned to check my alligator traps this morning, but my partner will take care of them this afternoon, so we won't be going past my traps after all."

"You're not taking out your boat because we were invited to go along, aren't you?" Justin asked.

"You're my excuse; you'll see soon enough." Armand grinned. "Grab the boat pole after you're in."

The three of them put on their vests before they climbed into the boat; Armand took his seat while Justin shoved the boat away from the bank using the pole.

Armand started up the engine.

Wren asked, "Is this what they call a putt-putt engine?"

Armand stared at her. "Sure is; it's compact and doesn't go too deep into the water, which is good because we need an engine that can skim us through the water hyacinths without getting tangled up. How'd you know about that?"

Wren smiled. "I wrote an article about shrimp fishing off the South Carolina coast for a sports magazine. I took a course in boating because the publisher didn't want me to come off as the landlubber that I was. The captain of the boat insisted I spend the four-month season with them, so I wouldn't have only a few hours of experience and think I was an expert. He was right; I started as a know-it-all and ended as a humbled boat hand."

Armand whistled low. "You want to take the helm?"

Wren shook her head. "No, I'd need a refresher; I'd probably be okay after a time or two of watching you."

Armand smiled. "Maybe we'll have a chance later for you to get some hands-on time."

Wren grinned. "I'd love it."

As Armand maneuvered the boat in a crawl along the channel of water, he pointed. "See that log next to the bank?"

Wren narrowed her eyes. "Yes."

Justin squinted. "It's got two bumps."

"That there's an alligator; they frequently lie low in the water like that with only the two bumps of their eyes giving them away."

Wren peered at the water alongside the boat. "I see fish close to the bottom."

"Probably catfish," Armand said. "We got us a cabin coming up in a short piece; let me know if anybody's waving, and we'll slow down to see if they need anything from the store."

As they rounded a small bend in the river, Armand slowed.

"I see someone on the porch," Wren said.

When they were close to the cabin, a woman who held a baby on her hip called out, "You goin' up river, Armand? Can you fetch me a five-pound sack of flour?"

"Will do."

"'Preciate you."

Armand waved; as he continued up the river, he furrowed his brow.

"What's wrong?" Justin asked.

Armand spoke softly as he maneuvered the channel. "I dropped off ten pounds of flour last week; she's got something to tell me she doesn't want other people hearing."

"Who would be around to hear?" Justin asked in a voice as quiet as Armand's.

Armand raised his eyebrows. "You saw the alligator."

"Alligator has eyes; bayou has ears?" Wren asked.

Armand smiled; after he cleared his throat, he spoke in a clear voice. "Good question, Wren; yep, that was a mockingbird you heard."

"Thanks." Wren glanced at Justin, who smiled and winked. *He understood what Armand said.*

As they continued toward their destination, Armand pointed out the plants by name along the bank and explained their uses in local recipes and folk medicine.

"I'll never remember all these names," Wren said.

Armand chuckled. "I practically grew up on the water. My grandpa and I cruised the bayou and fished in his small boat on days when I didn't go to school; he'd point out the plants and tell me what they were and how they were used until I could tell him. He said as long as we brought home a big ole mess of catfish, nobody cared how long we were gone."

After a few more miles of twists and bends in the bayou, Wren said, "I'm all turned around, but aren't we going back the way we came?"

"Feels like it, doesn't it?" Armand chuckled. "We're coming up to the secret hideout Grandpa and I built. If we were on the bayou and got hit by a sudden downpour or the fish weren't biting, but we didn't want to go home, we'd stay in our hideout shack and play cards. He taught me how to play boo-ray."

"I've never heard of it," Justin said.

"It's kind of like the card game of spades is the best way I can explain it, except you play with poker chips, and the rules are pretty fluid and can change from game to game and sometimes in the middle of the game, it seems to me. Grandpa taught me some really neat sleight-of-hand tricks, and we'd try to catch each other cheating; by the time I was seven years old, I was pretty good at it."

"Your grandpa taught you how to cheat at cards?" Wren side-glanced at Justin, who rubbed his chin to hide his growing smile.

"Yep, and more important, how to spot a cheater; I've dropped out of many a game before I lost all my money."

"That's definitely a handy skill to have," Justin said.

"Yep; Grandpa said to first look at their hands and hair before you sat down to play. If their fingernails were clean, and they had a store-bought haircut, you was dealing with a grifter. The only thing to do was announce you heard your mama calling and leave."

"I'm going to remember that," Justin said.

Armand deftly steered the small boat into a tiny cove sheltered by swamp willows.

Wren glanced at the swamp willows and the bushes with tiny pink flowers that grew alongside the trees. "This is really beautiful; it's like a fairyland."

"It's private and peaceful; always been a comfort to me."

After they stepped out of the boat, Wren frowned. "Where's the shed?"

"Not ten feet from where you're standing." Armand grinned.

Wren and Justin followed him past the trees; when he stopped and pointed, Wren gasped. "We were practically on top of it. Did you hide your boat while you played cards?"

"Sure did; pulled it into the trees."

As they headed back to the boat, Wren said, "Did you and your grandpa ever give your private place a name?"

"We called it the fishing hole."

After they climbed into the boat, Justin said, "We need a fishing hole, honey."

"We'll be in the middle of the desert, Justin; who will believe we have a fishing hole?" Wren tilted her head.

"None of their business." Justin winked.

Armand chuckled as he started up the engine. "You got the right idea, Justin."

As they left the fishing hole, Wren tried to remember the trees and the bank. "I can't see it anymore, Armand; how can you find it so easily?"

"Just like I know the names of all them plants; you see something three or so times a week your entire life, and you just know."

After a few more turns, Armand said, "Keep watching because we're fixing to come up on an authentic Cajun general store and diner."

When they took what seemed to be a random side channel off the bayou, Justin pointed to a dock. "Looks like we're here."

After Armand secured the small boat, Justin climbed out before he helped Wren out of the boat. As the three of them made their way down a narrow path through the trees, Justin inhaled. "Something's cooking, and it smells good."

When they came to a clearing, Wren's eyes widened at the substantial log structure with bright yellow, green, and white checked curtains in the window and a sign across the top of the porch, "Welcome to the Mud Bug Outpost."

"The original Mud Bug Outpost was a shack that sold provisions to the folks and was the first point of alarm and protection for a nearby settlement from bayou raiders, but the building burned down years ago," Armand said as they strolled to the store. "In the old days, it was the only convenient and reliable source folks around here had for food and other staples. When the new owners who bought the Cranky Crawfish Café down the road a piece forty years ago heard about the Mud Bug, they bought the land and built a replica of the old outpost. The Mud Bug Outpost is twenty miles away by road from the Cranky Crawfish Café, but you can get there by boat in fifteen minutes if you know the bayou as well as our long-term residents do."

Wren glanced at the mirror next to the door and a box of brightly painted pebbles in a box on the porch.

As Armand opened the door, she furrowed her brow. *The campground office had a mirror and a box of marbles.*

When they went inside, all conversations suddenly ceased; the three men who were sitting at the counter turned to look at them. Justin nodded as Armand said, "Hey, boys. How are y'all doing?"

Before any of the men replied, a young woman called out, "Armand, I expected you here an hour ago; if you can't be any more timely than that, our wedding is off."

The men at the counter chuckled and turned back to their coffee while the rest of the diners resumed their noisy conversations.

"There you go, honey; breaking my heart once again." Armand grinned as he hurried to kiss her on the cheek. "Are we good now?" He patted her behind.

She swatted his arm. "None of that, boyfriend, until I get my ring blessed by the priest, and we exchange our vows in front of our families; I suppose you're too rude to introduce me, so I'll have to do it myself." She held out her hand. "My mother named me Magnolia, but everybody calls me Mags."

"I'm Wren, and this is Justin." Wren shook Mags' hand.

"Nice to meet you," Justin added as he shook with Mags.

"I'll bring three coffees and menus; sit wherever you can find a spot. Anyone care for café au lait?"

Wren shook her head.

"None for us," Justin said.

After they found a table, Mags poured their coffee and handed them menus; her dark eyes twinkled. "If you want a regular American breakfast of greasy fried eggs, frozen hash brown potatoes, and burnt white bread toast, we can do that, but we'll massively overcharge you for it. You having your usual crawfish and egg scramble, Armand?"

Armand nodded. "No sense in changing gears now."

While Wren studied the menu, Justin said, "The Andouille sausage and sweet potato hash topped with a poached egg has my name written all over it."

"Wren, are you having trouble deciding? I'll bring you the petite-sized breakfast of shrimp and grits."

"And a beignet?" Wren asked.

"Absolutely." Mags refilled their cups then shouted out their order over the din as she refilled cups on her way to drop off the ticket.

"Are you going to share your beignet with me?" Justin asked.

"She is not," Mags called out over the noise in the small café while she handed a man his change at the cash register. "You're getting your own, mister."

"I should have warned you that nothing gets past Mags," Armand leaned over the table to speak quietly to Justin.

When Mags brought their food, she set Armand's plate in front of him with a thud. "And don't you forget it either, bud."

Before she left, she smiled at Wren and Justin. "You two are the cutest couple ever, aren't they, Armand?"

"Nowhere as cute as you are, sha," Armand said.

When Justin furrowed his brow, Wren whispered, "Sha is like saying sweetie; it's the Cajun way of pronouncing 'cher'."

Mags grabbed up a menu from the next table and fanned her face. "Love them fancy words of yours, Armand." Her cheeks reddened as she hurried away for the next order.

While they were eating, Armand whispered, "Where's Mags?"

"Behind you; up by the cash register," Wren whispered.

Armand's mouth twitched into a smile as he spoke even more softly. "Do you think she'd approve of a wedding two weeks from Friday?"

Wren and Justin laughed as Mags lifted both hands over her head with her thumbs up. Wren put her thumbs up, and Armand grinned.

When Mags came to their table with hot beignets straight from the fryer, she asked, "Are y'all going to be around this Friday? Armand, bring them to the catfish fry and engagement party."

She leaned over and kissed Armand, and the customers erupted in cheers and wolf whistles. She sashayed to the cash register then put her hand on her hip as she glanced over her shoulder at Armand and flipped her hair. Armand grinned as he and Justin high-fived, and the crowd roared.

A tall, wiry man with gray streaks in his military style haircut and the bearing of an officer approached their table. After Armand introduced the man to Justin and Wren, the man said, "Marshal, your colleague planned to be here, but he's been detained. Do you have time for a phone call?"

Justin rose. "I won't be long, honey."

"We'll wait for you by the boat," Armand said.

Justin followed the old man to the door.

When the door closed behind the two men, Armand asked, "Ready, Wren?"

As they headed toward the cash register, Mags briefly stroked Armand's arm with her fingertips as he passed her. "Be safe."

He nodded. "Number one on my plan for the day, sha."

Wren followed Armand to the general store side of the Mud Bug Outpost. While he shopped for flour, Wren examined the ball caps with the Mud Bug Outpost logo. After she put on a rustic olive cap, she peered into the sliver of a mirror next to the sunglasses display and glimpsed someone staring at her.

When Wren wheeled around, no one was there.

She pursed her lips and shook her head. *It must have been a display photo. I'm not usually this jumpy.*

After she picked out a camouflage cap for Justin, Wren hurried to check out behind Armand.

Armand smiled. "Good choices, Wren."

On their way to the boat, Wren said, "I've never had so much fun at breakfast, and the food was fantastic."

"It is the best, isn't it? Thanks for your help with Mags; I've been trying to nail her down on a wedding date for months, and she always tells me she's thinking about it."

"How did I help?" Wren asked.

"It's the way you and Justin look at each other; Mags has had this idea that there's no such thing as people made for each other like we are, but you two are living proof. She's been looking for a reason to set a date." Armand shrugged. "I'll never understand you women, but I guess I don't have to, do I?"

"Justin and I are that obvious?" Wren asked.

"Like a big ole flashing neon sign."

When they stopped near the boat, Wren peered at the water then side-glanced at Armand. "There seems to be an undercurrent that I didn't notice before."

Armand narrowed his eyes. "You're not talking about the water, are you? Babette told me you don't miss much."

As Justin hurried on the path toward them, Armand shook his head. "Be careful who you trust, Wren; the bayou is treacherous."

"What am I missing?"

"Tell Babette about the fishing hole."

Wren furrowed her brow as she put on her life vest. *If I don't miss much, what all did I just miss?*

Justin kissed Wren when he joined them. "I didn't mean to be gone so long."

"We just got here," Armand said. "Get your vest on, and we'll push off."

After they were headed down the bayou, Justin said, "I like your new ball cap, Wren."

"That's good because I got one for you too." She pulled out his ball cap from her backpack.

Justin chuckled as he examined his cap. "Camo and a cranky crawfish; it's great."

When he put it on, Wren said, "Looks good."

Justin posed with his arm propped on the side of the boat as he lifted his chin and gazed across the bayou.

Wren giggled. "Downright sexy, Marshal."

"You're a Cajun *cou-za* now, Justin; welcome to the family." Armand's eyes twinkled. "That's pronounced cousin in Arizona lingo, Wren."

Armand steered the boat toward the bank in front of the cabin where the young woman had hailed him. "Delivery time," he said.

After they climbed out of the boat, Armand said, "Stay with the boat, cousin; there's nowhere to tie it up, and I don't feel like swimming with the alligators if it slips away."

Justin smiled. "I'll hang onto it; I didn't plan on a swim today, either."

"Want to come see the baby, Wren?" Armand asked.

Wren blinked. "I'd love to."

Armand raised an eyebrow. "You can hold the baby while we talk."

"Of course."

When they neared the cabin, the young woman stepped out on the porch with her baby on her hip and an old gray spotted coon hound at her side. Wren raised her eyebrows. *The cabin has a mirror on the wall next to the door and a small box with rocks in it just like the registration office.*

"You're such a cutie." Wren smiled at the baby and cooed as she stepped onto the porch. When Wren made a popping sound with her mouth, the baby chortled. Wren held out her hands, and the baby reached for her.

The young woman laughed. "Okay, buddy. I know how much you like your older women."

# Chapter Four

While Wren swayed with the baby, he watched her face with fascination when she made faces and silly sounds.

She stepped to the other side of the porch and turned her back to Armand and the young woman, ostensibly to give them privacy, so they could speak without being overheard.

The baby tried to mimic Wren's facial expressions as she continued with nonsense sounds and slowly repeated her best baby-entertaining routine of raising her eyebrows, blinking, puckering her lips, wiggling her eyebrows, and twitching her mouth.

Armand spoke softly. "Don't worry; she's focused on the baby."

The woman exhaled. "You're right; she's got the baby fever."

*Baby fever? Whatever works.* Wren smiled, and the baby copied her.

"You're such a cutie patootie," Wren whispered. The baby giggled.

"So tell me what's going on," Armand said.

"Have you heard of the new Lilith?"

"No," Armand said.

"She claims to be Tante Julia Brown reincarnated or some such; most people say she's Pere Malfait's wife; others whisper she's a rougarou. She charges for what she calls protection, but it's blackmail. Terrible things happen to those who refuse to pay. This week, she doubled our weekly protection payment; my husband already has a second job; now he's looking for a third one, but I don't know when he'll sleep." The woman's voice cracked. "I don't know how we'll pay this week."

"We can help you; call Babette and tell her how much you need, and she'll get it to you. What else can we do?"

"Stop Lilith," the young woman growled.

"What do we know about her? Who has seen her?" Armand asked.

"I don't know who she is or where she came from; I don't know who has seen her, but nobody talks about her if anyone is around. We get texts from a private number or find notes on our porch in the mornings, but our dog never barks; she's a sweet old girl and howls when she trees a raccoon, but only barks when there's a threat."

"Does that mean somebody she knows is dropping off the notes?"

"More than likely, but I've never known her to bark at a woman. She knew you, but not Wren."

"Anything else you can think of that will help me?" Armand asked.

"I hadn't thought of it before, but Lilith seems to know everyone and everything, so she isn't an outsider."

Armand exhaled. "Wren, are you ready to go?"

Wren pretended to sneeze, and the baby giggled, so she did it again.

The baby's mama joined Wren. "Is Miss Wren funny?" she cooed.

Wren smiled as she handed the baby to his mother. "We were having fun."

"You certainly were," the young woman beamed.

"Ready to go, Wren?" Armand asked as the young mother carried her baby and called the dog as she went inside.

While they strolled away from the cabin, Armand said, "I took a chance when I asked if you were ready to go the first time, but you caught right on. I knew I could trust you to catch on. I'll keep Babette posted if I learn anything new, and you can tell Justin for me. You won't see me for a while because I've picked up some extra construction work; I've been a little too high profile as it is this morning."

When they joined Justin at the boat, he said, "Two kayaks went by; I stayed in the shadows, but they never even glanced my way. I'm seeing how difficult it would be to find anyone hiding in the bayou."

After they returned to the dock near the campground, Armand shook hands with Justin and Wren. "Nice to meet you two; I'll check in with Babette to let her know when I'll be picking you up for the engagement party on Friday; be sure to bring your appetite. Oh, one more thing, Justin."

"I'm going to pick up Rascal," Wren said.

Before she reached the office, Justin caught up with her.

"What's up?" she asked.

"We'll talk after we pick up Rascal."

When they went into the office, Rascal scrambled to greet them. While Wren hugged Rascal, Babette asked, "How was breakfast?"

"It was great," Wren said. "I'm not sure I'll be able to eat anything before tomorrow, though."

Babette smiled. "The cook always says if you leave there hungry, it's your own dang fault."

"We were totally guiltless then," Wren returned Babette's smile. "Armand said I should tell you he took us to the fishing hole; is that important?"

Babette raised her eyebrows. "It's very important; it means he trusts you two, so I can too. These are times when it's critical to be careful who you trust."

"I didn't want to embarrass myself, but I heard some things I didn't understand," Wren said.

"I thought it was just me." Justin smiled at Wren.

"Who is Pere Malfait and what is a rougarou?" Wren asked.

Babette shuddered. "Pere Malfait is pure evil, like the devil; rougarou is a werewolf."

Wren nodded. "I noticed you have a mirror outside the door and a box on the porch with marbles in it. They seemed like strange porch decorations."

Babette smiled. "Not around here; you'll find them at almost any Cajun home or establishment. The mirror is for Pere Malfait; he's so vain that before he enters a house to cause trouble, he stops to admire himself. He's so enamored by his appearance that he stands in front of the mirror until dawn when the sunbeams chase him away. The rougarou is obsessed with counting but can't count higher than twelve. All the boxes have thirteen items in them. When the rougarou gets to the thirteenth item, she loses track of her count and has to start over. When the sun comes up, she disappears. What else?"

"Would the rougarou be Pere Malfait's wife?" Wren asked.

"Not at all; if Pere Malfait had a wife, it would be Lilith because she represents death, destruction, and evil. You're definitely becoming immersed in the Cajun culture, Wren."

"It's so rich that I could feel it all around me as we traveled the channel in the bayou," Wren said. "I owe my editor a blog today, so I'm soaking in everything I can."

On the way to the camper, Wren asked, "What's up, Justin?"

"I thought we'd wait until we were in the trailer to talk, so it would be private."

Rascal raced ahead and waited for them at the picnic table.

After they were inside, Wren sat on the sofa and watched while Justin paced as he talked.

"Armand caught me up on the conversation at the cabin. When I went outside at the Mud Bug, I called the local sheriff, Victor Landry. He asked me to appear on a panel at a law enforcement conference in New Orleans tomorrow; he's the moderator for the panel, and one of his key panelists dropped out this morning because of illness. The conference begins with a social this evening and ends the day after tomorrow with a luncheon. It's an excellent opportunity for me professionally, but Sheriff Landry and I would have to leave this afternoon and wouldn't return until after the luncheon. I told him I couldn't leave you, but I realized I was making a decision that affected both of us without letting you know."

"You'd be helping a colleague, and it would be good for you professionally, so why wouldn't you go?"

Justin crossed his arms. "Because after what Armand said, I don't want to be away from you."

"Are you finished pacing?" Wren patted the sofa next to her.

Justin sat next to her and put his arm around Wren's shoulders while she talked. "I have the luxurious fifth wheel with a bathroom, and this is a wonderful campground; I already have friends I can trust. We'll be apart for only a day and a half. I'll have Rascal, and my powder is dry. You almost left me out of the decision, so you'll owe me another I'm sorry kiss and maybe a beignet when you return."

Justin hugged her and exhaled. "You're trying to distract me with logic; I should stay."

Wren glared at him. "You're going to stay in case of what? And let a friend down? That doesn't sound like you at all. What are you going to wear?"

"You are so practical; I have my uniform with me for tomorrow; Vic said the social and the luncheon are informal, so I can wear jeans and a nice shirt."

"Do you want me to help you pack? I've done a lot more traveling than you have. Where will you stay?"

Justin gave Wren an extra squeeze. "The packing is simple, so I can handle it; the other panelist's room at the conference hotel is available for me. I'll text you all the information after I get there."

"Do you know what the panel topic is?" Wren asked.

Justin pulled her closer and nuzzled her neck then nibbled on her ear and whispered, "Tell me more about how sexy I am."

Wren giggled and pulled up her shoulder. "Don't change the subject; that tickles."

"I know, but you're fun. The official title is long, but it is essentially a panel on the challenges of law enforcement staffing in rural areas. Vic told me he'd explain why it has become a hot topic on our way to New Orleans. He's driving."

"Do you still plan to worry about the extortion along the bayou the entire time you're gone?"

"The sheriff told me he'd heard about quite a few people but didn't have anything firsthand until they received a tip late last night; I'll let him know the extortionist is still active in case the lead they are working on doesn't pan out." Justin traced her bottom lip with the tip of his finger.

"It's going to be a long day and a half." Wren leaned against him.

Justin leaned down and kissed her lightly.

Wren sighed. "I could go with you, but Rascal and I are not hotel people."

Justin laughed. "Neither am I, honey. I might have to call for hotel etiquette advice."

"I'm not the right one to ask, but I'll bet we'd come up with something creative. Send me a selfie."

"Hey, that's my line." Justin gave her a quick peck on the cheek then hurried to his bedroom. "I have to pack; I'm sorry you and Rascal can't go with me."

"Rascal probably could, but I'd pull a chair out into the hallway, so I could watch people while they got off the elevator to see what kind of luggage they had."

Justin laughed. "I can see you doing it too. I'll send you a selfie of me and the elevator."

Wren opened her laptop after she sat in her recliner and put up her feet.

"Are you going to blog? Rascal and I will go to the dog park or maybe walk the trail; one of us has excess nervous energy."

"That's a great idea; I'd like to go along. I can blog after you leave."

As they walked along the trail of crushed stone, Rascal bolted ahead then raced back to check in.

When Rascal dashed away again, Wren said, "This is a great trail for Rascal and for me. My knee and ankle are fine now, but I'm still a little afraid of falling."

"I know the cure for that." Justin took her hand, and they strolled along together as a mockingbird serenaded them.

Wren glanced at the clear sky. "Looks like your travel weather will be nice; driving in rainstorms is not my favorite."

"I guess not with all the road traveling you've done. I'm still amazed at how many miles you and Rascal have traveled this past month. Will you miss traveling?"

"If I do, we have the fifth wheel and can go camping for a weekend or a few days. By the time we reach Arizona, I'll be cured of any urge to take a long trip for quite a while."

When they rounded a corner, Rascal barked a warning as he dashed back to them.

"What is it, Rascal?" Wren asked. Rascal faced the trail ahead of them and growled.

"Stay right here; I'll check real quick." Justin trotted ahead and disappeared around a curve; a few seconds later, he reappeared.

"Good boy, Rascal." Justin scratched Rascal's ears. "Wren, there's an alligator lounging in a sunny spot in the middle of the path. We might want to skip the trail this morning."

When they turned back toward their trailer, Rascal yipped and ran ahead.

"Do me a huge favor and don't go on the trail while I'm gone," Justin said. "It's Louisiana; the alligators were here first, so we'll give them priority on the trail."

"Agreed." Wren shuddered.

When they returned to the campground, Justin said, "Let's spend a little time at the dog park and watch the last-minute exodus of those who are checking out this morning."

Wren giggled. "We can be judgy while we see who prepared the night before to leave today, and who prefers to wait until the last possible minute."

Justin opened the dog park gate for Rascal, who trotted inside. "Do people really do that? Watch the other campers?"

"All the time, but they're polite and don't stare," Wren said.

While they surreptitiously watched the nearby campers prepare to leave, Justin said, "I'm actually learning a few pointers. Do you already know all this stuff? This would be excellent surveillance training for a rookie deputy; I'll have to mention it to Pat except we couldn't practice it at the Forgotten Oasis Campground because Betsy would explain what was going on to each new guest upon arrival."

Wren giggled. "That's exactly what Betsy would do because she'd be so proud of the campground being the training ground for new deputies. That's something else I can do this afternoon: I'll call Betsy after I send the blog to Kendra."

After they returned to the trailer and had lunch, Justin's phone buzzed a text. "Vic's on his way. Are you sure you'll be okay? I can still cancel," Justin said.

"I'd feel awful if you did," Wren said. "You're really only going to be gone for one whole day, and that's tomorrow."

"You're right." Justin exhaled and rubbed Rascal's ears. "Take care of our girl, Rascal."

When the sheriff pulled in front of the trailer in his cruiser, Justin kissed Wren. "I love you, sweetie."

After he grabbed his gear, he left.

Wren sighed. "I miss him already, but I couldn't tell him that, Rascal."

Rascal nudged Wren's arm, and she stroked his back.

After she wrote half a page, her phone buzzed a text. She frowned as she read it. "Babette wants us to come to the office, Rascal."

When Wren and Rascal reached the office, Babette was sobbing as she opened the door for them.

"Wren, the police searched Tante Simone's house on an anonymous tip and discovered drugs; now Tante Penelope has disappeared."

"Penelope is Simone's sister, right?"

Babette nodded. "Armand told me you know about the extortionist using the name Lilith. I've taken on a night job for extra money to help a friend until Lilith is stopped. A long-time resident of the bayou, Naomi Boudreaux, will fill in for me in the afternoons. She has managed the campground for me a few times on weekends when I've gone out of town, so she's familiar with how we do things. She used to work for the parish planning department, but she retired not too long ago. Naomi doesn't know about the fishing hole; she's a hard worker, but she doesn't have any filters."

"Parish?" Wren asked.

Babette smiled. "It's like a Georgia county."

"I didn't know, thanks. I'll be careful what I say to Naomi. What can I do for you?"

"Keep yourself safe and be just another campground guest."

"There has to be more I can do as an innocent campground guest," Wren said.

"If anything comes up, we'll mention the fishing hole, so you'll know it's us; is it okay if I give Armand your cell phone number? I'll be here in the morning."

"That's fine. Does Mags know about the fishing hole?"

"No, Armand has been careful to keep her insulated because she'd charge right in, knocking heads together and taking names." Babette rolled her eyes. "Armand did a little digging and discovered the extortion hadn't extended to the Mud Bug or the Cranky Crawfish, so he's certain she's okay. It's Mags' nature to flirt, so the flirtation between Mags and Armand has been a running joke for a long time." Babette's smile was weak. "When they realized they were serious about each other after all, they kept up the joke because that's how they are. Most of the crowd that will show up Friday at the engagement party for a big laugh will pretend they knew all along that Mags and Armand were serious."

"Even though I've only spent a short amount of time with the two of them, I can imagine them loving a good joke," Wren said.

"That's how they are. My brother used to drive me crazy when we were growing up because he was such a tease, but he met his match in Mags; I love it."

Before Wren left, Babette hugged her. "You're a good person, Wren."

Rascal trotted alongside Wren; when she opened the door to the trailer, he leaped inside without touching the steps.

"That was impressive." Wren closed the door and sat at the table with her laptop. "Blog first."

When she was wrapping up the ending of her blog, her phone buzzed a text from Justin.

"Miss you. Sorry we couldn't have taken the trailer and stayed in the hotel parking lot. Love you."

Wren giggled as she replied, "Can you imagine? See you on Friday. We can celebrate with a party. Love you too."

Wren sighed and wrapped up her blog. Rascal whined when she closed her laptop.

"Both of us could use a break. Let's walk around the campground and check out our new neighbors before we go to the dog park."

Wren picked up Rascal's leash and wrapped it like a lasso. "There are more trailers and RVs than we've been used to this trip; I'll carry this for show."

As they neared a trailer, a toddler squealed and raced from the campsite toward Rascal while her mother shouted as she chased the little one, "No, no. Leave the doggie alone."

Wren stopped, and Rascal stayed close to her side. When the toddler neared them, Rascal yipped.

The little girl stopped and pointed at him. "Doggie. Sit, doggie."

Rascal grinned and sat.

The little girl's mother slowed to a walk and took her daughter's hand when she caught up with her. "I'd swear your dog told her to stop."

Wren smiled. "Rascal caught her attention; he's patient with little ones."

"Thank you, Rascal; she gets away from me so fast sometimes."

"She did look like she was on a mission."

"Can we say hello to Rascal?" the mother asked.

"Sure; tell her to stop before she gets too close, so he can sniff her. That will work with friendly dogs; you can always ask if the dog likes toddlers. Dog people will tell you."

The woman nodded. "The doggie wants to sniff you; that's how doggies say hello."

When the mother and little girl were close, Rascal leaned toward the toddler and sniffed. The little one sniffed Rascal. "Doggie."

"He does smell like a doggie, doesn't he? You smell like a little girl." Wren smiled.

"Let's go back to our trailer now. What do you say to the doggie?"

"Thank you, doggie."

Before she turned, the woman said, "My husband always had a big dog when he was a kid and has been wanting a Labrador Retriever, but I've never been around dogs and thought a smaller dog would be better with a little one. Are they all like Rascal?"

"I know I'm prejudiced, but Labrador Retrievers are the best dogs in the world for kids; I'll bet your husband will be your best advisor."

The woman held onto the toddler's hand while they headed to their trailer; the little one jumped and sang, "Doggie, doggie, doggie."

"You've got a fan, Rascal." Wren opened the dog park gate.

Rascal found a tennis ball and dropped it in the box with dog toys near the gate. While he checked the rest of the dog park for more forgotten toys, Wren's phone buzzed a text from Betsy. "Call when you aren't busy; no rush."

Rascal trotted to Wren and leaned against her. While she rubbed his face and stroked his back, Wren smiled. *I'll call her later; Rascal and I are busy.*

After they returned to the trailer, Wren called Betsy.

"I almost called you when you didn't call me right back. Where are you?"

"Rascal and I were at the dog park, but we're back in the camper now. What's up?"

"Was I supposed to remind you to blog? Isn't the blog due this week?"

"No, Kendra keeps up with the schedule. The blog is due next week, but I'm working on it today, so Gage will have time to publish it without being rushed."

"Good; Socorro is busy planning a surprise party. She's keeping it hush-hush; I don't even know the details. I think it's a welcome to Hidden Gulch for the new teacher and his wife. When are you going to be back? Socorro said she would ask you, but I can save her the trouble. I'm certain she intends for you to be here for the party."

"It's nice of her to include me, but I have a new article to write; did I forget to tell you?"

"It's more likely that I forgot." Betsy chuckled. "That's okay; maybe we can have a welcome home party for you, except it will only be us. Speaking of which, do you know what Justin is working on? I haven't seen him since Sunday, or maybe it was Monday. When I saw Pat in the grocery store yesterday, I asked him about Justin, but he didn't answer me. I don't think he heard me; we're all getting a little older, aren't we? Not you, though."

"Well, Justin is..."

Betsy continued, "Always busy, isn't he? You know about the patio at the campground, right? Did you know Socorro has enclosed it? It's almost finished; she wanted to have the outdoor look but still be cool in the summer and warm at night when our temperatures drop, and she has pulled it off. Socorro found three food trucks that have committed to rotating Saturdays; she's planning a grand opening after you're here because we wouldn't be doing all this if it hadn't been for you. You won't recognize the campground. Socorro and Sheridan have been expanding and upgrading it, except Socorro won't allow any upgrades to the old saloon except for the few boards that Sheridan replaced; I never thought she'd be so sentimental about a hundred-year-old building that's practically a skeleton. I gotta go. Two enormous RVs pulled in; we've been really busy since your article about the campground was published in the travel magazine." Betsy hung up.

"Sometimes I wonder why I don't tell Betsy that Justin is here, but when I try, she doesn't slow down at all. Maybe she'll settle down after we're in Hidden Gulch, Rascal."

Rascal yipped.

"I doubt it too, but every time she calls, I'm reminded how much Hidden Gulch is my home."

Wren sat at the table and reviewed her blog. After she sent it to Kendra, she exhaled. "That felt good. I'm inspired to work on my Cypress Knees Campground article."

After an hour, Wren stretched and read what she had written. "I don't like this at all, Rascal. All I've done is rewrite the story Simone told." She shrugged. "Maybe it helped after all; I got the back story out of my system, so now I can focus on the campground."

Wren wrote half a page. "I wonder if Naomi could give me some insights about the campground. Want to go to the office, Rascal?"

When they went into the office, Rascal growled; Wren frowned as she shushed him.

A tall, muscular, middle-aged woman with dark skin and a bright turquoise turban that covered her hair smiled. "You must be Wren and Rascal. I have cats, Wren, so I'm used to not being so popular with the dogs. No offense taken, Rascal. What can I do for you, Wren?"

Wren opened the door for Rascal, who went outside and sat on the porch.

# Chapter Five

"I'm writing an article about the campground for a travel magazine. I was wondering if you could tell me anything about it."

"Of course. Why don't you sit at the table if you'd like to take notes?"

After Wren sat at the table, she pulled out a spiral notebook and pen.

"Where would you like for me to start?" Naomi asked.

"I'm impressed with how well-kept it is; has it always been that way?"

Naomi chuckled. "Not at all. The previous owner was elderly and ill and no longer able to care for the campground. Several people from town formed an association to buy the campground. They decided we wanted it run by locals, and Armand and Babette's parents were interested, so the association loaned them the money to buy it before Babette was born. Babette's mother has a green thumb, and her father is what you'd call a master handyman. They fixed up the campground and paid off the loan five or six years ago and retired. The Dupre family still owns it, but Babette runs it. When the folks pass on, it will go to Babette and Armand. Babette manages it and takes care of the landscaping; Armand takes care of the maintenance, which works for him because he doesn't have to punch a clock."

"What can you tell me about the rumors the campground is haunted because people hear wailing at night when the wind blows?"

"It's the charm of the campground, and the idea of being haunted is intriguing to people, so no one discourages repeating the tale."

"Do you think it's haunted?"

Wren smiled at Naomi's deep-throated chuckle. "It doesn't matter what I think; it's always been a part of the mystique of the campground. We could go outside right now and hear sounds in the trees when the wind blows even lightly. Night sounds carry better because it's quieter than it is in the daytime, but please don't let my logical nature color your article. If our guests want to come here and be thrilled by the sounds from long ago in the trees, then I'm excited for them; Babette wants them to enjoy their visit, so that's what I want."

"How did the original idea of the haunting sounds start?"

"It was long before the Dupres bought the campground. My theory is that as the campground became more and more rundown, people thought of it as creepy; if you add the whistling trees, you have a haunted campground. To their credit, the Dupres were business savvy when they used that as a marketing draw. It's been very effective. I'm sure you've seen the website. It has a creepy vibe to it, don't you think?"

"The website is impressive; it hints of Louisiana's history of voodoo without being blatant, and several of the reviews mentioned the campground was haunted."

"Right after they bought the campground, Babette's mother would tell a few people who were using the laundry her story she'd made up about the campground being haunted."

"That's perfect. Does anyone remember the story?"

"Babette wrote a paper based on the story for her high school history class. The teacher gave Babette a low grade because the teacher claimed it was fantasy, not history; he was an idiot and didn't last long at the school. I'm sure Babette's mother still has a copy. Should I call her and ask?"

"I don't want to put you to any trouble," Wren said.

"No trouble at all; give me a second." Naomi picked up her phone. After listening for a few moments, Naomi said, "She didn't answer; I'll call again later and let you know when I have a copy."

"I'd be happy to pick it up," Wren said.

Naomi chuckled. "You don't want to do that; they bought a ranch in Montana when they retired. I understand that ranching is hard work and not what most people would consider as a retirement plan, but that's the Dupres for you. She'll probably email it to me. Shall I print it for you, or would you rather I forward it to your phone or email?"

"I'll give you my email address; if you sent it to my phone, I'd have to forward it to my email." Naomi handed Wren a notepad and a pen.

Wren wrote her email address she used for her blog.

Naomi frowned as she looked at the address. "This is different."

"It's my blog email, and the one I check most frequently. My personal email has turned into an ads bucket. I never check it anymore."

Naomi smiled. "You young people are so smart these days. I get those ads, and I've never figured out how to delete them; I spend most of my email time trying to find any emails I want to read."

Wren returned her smile. "I know, right?"

When Wren closed the door behind her, she raised her eyebrows at Rascal, who had stretched out in a sunbeam that hit the porch. "You look relaxed; was it really her cats that bothered you?"

Rascal grunted.

"I didn't think so, but I kind of took the hint and didn't give her my phone number. Want to do a little exploring?"

Wren and Rascal walked toward the cabin then followed the road to the next cabin. When they came to the end of the road, Wren examined the wide path on their left. "That looks like a service road. Do you feel adventuresome?"

Rascal grinned and bounded ahead then waited for Wren until she caught up. After they passed the firepit, they came to the dog park.

"That was fun, wasn't it?" As they strolled to the camper, Wren continued, "Of course, now that I gave Naomi the blog email address, I have to check it. I better do that now in case I need to ask Gage to reset my password, since I don't remember checking it since he first set it up."

After they returned to the trailer, Wren checked her passwords. "I actually have a password, but I don't know how I get to the admin part of the website or whatever I need to do. Maybe I have the link somewhere else."

While she searched for the link, her phone buzzed a text from Justin. "We're here; the room is comfortable. We ran into heavier than expected traffic, so we'll need to go to the meeting room in half an hour. Love you."

Wren sighed. "Love you too. Enjoy your evening. Call me whenever you get back to your room."

Wren sent Gage a text. "I have my password, but how do I get into my email?"

Gage immediately responded with a link.

Wren clicked on the link and entered her email and password.

"Gage has been keeping up with my email, Rascal." She checked the sent messages and giggled. "He signs his emails as Senior Executive Nice Guy. I wonder if Tara knows about that; although, the last we heard, Tara had forgiven him for his destructive behavior."

Wren's phone rang.

"Hey, it's Gage. Are you going to be checking your email regularly now?"

"No, not for a while." Wren told him about Justin, Charlie, the fifth wheel, and one more travel article.

"Mom knows about the article, right?" Gage asked.

"Yes. She was the first person I called."

"You don't have to tell me anything, but does Mom approve of the sleeping arrangements?"

Wren rolled her eyes. "Yes; separate bedrooms, Mr. Nosy Nice Guy."

"Ha, you saw it; what did you think? Tara told me she thinks I'm goofy, but that's a step up from being a terrible person. Why are you suddenly using your website email?"

"Your new title made me laugh. Someone asked for my phone number or email. She's a very pleasant woman, but Rascal didn't take to her at all; she said it was because she had cats, but I've never known Rascal to have a cat problem, so I gave her my blog email."

"Whoa, if Rascal didn't like her, there has to be a reason. I'm notified when emails come in, so I'll text you when I see it; it sounds like she doesn't deserve a response from Mr. Nice Guy, so I'll stay out unless I hear differently from you."

Wren giggled after she hung up. "Gage is still Gage, except he's genuinely enjoyable and not phony."

Wren opened the refrigerator then closed it. "I need to learn how to plan meals." She opened the freezer. "Thank goodness, I know how to cook pizza. I don't have my little combo air fryer and toaster oven anymore, and I'm not sure how to work the oven because I didn't get a walk-through. This might be tricky."

A plastic grocery sack and its contents were on top of the pizza, so she set the sack on the rack below and removed the frozen pizza.

Wren searched through the manuals that came with the trailer until she found one for the oven and burners. When she read the instructions on how to light the oven, she said, "This doesn't look nearly as hard as other ovens I've seen. I know the gas is on because we have hot water, and if we run out, I know how to switch bottles."

"Here we go." Wren pushed in the dial and turned the striker; when the gas was lit, she continued to hold down the dial. "Do you think it's okay to let go now?"

Rascal yipped; she slowly turned the dial to 450 degrees. After the oven reached temperature, Wren set the pizza on the rack in the oven. "At least I don't have to rotate or flip it."

After she set the timer, she fed Rascal.

She stared at the timer that seemed to move incredibly slowly as it counted down the minutes. While she waited, she pulled out a cutting board, a wide spatula, and the pizza cutter.

After Rascal finished eating, Wren picked up his food bowl and refilled his water dish before she put a fork, knife, and paper towel on the table.

When the timer went off, she peeked in the oven. "Maybe one more minute."

After the minute was up, she turned off the oven and used the spatula to slide the pizza onto the cutting board. She cut the pizza into quarters then cut one quarter in half.

She sat at the table with her two slices of pizza and moaned. "I need a drink and crushed red pepper."

When she opened the refrigerator, the jug of water was empty. *I forgot to refill it.* She filled the jug, placed it in the refrigerator and ran not quite cold water into a glass. She set her glass on the table but caught herself as she was about to sit down. *Crushed red pepper.*

She took a bite of her lukewarm pizza and sipped her lukewarm glass of water. After she finished eating, she wrapped the pizza in aluminum foil and put it in the refrigerator.

"Rascal, I also need to work on the timing for meals; I cooked only one thing and didn't sit down to a hot meal. I'd say I've never had this problem before, but I've always had incredible friends who were far more skilled at cooking that I am. At least I have lunch and supper taken care of for tomorrow, and when I need a break, I'm going to review the recipes everyone has sent me."

Rascal whined to go out. The moment Wren opened the door she heard someone tuning a fiddle, and she grabbed her backpack. Desirada hobbled toward her camper. "Come on, girl; Al's warming up his fiddle, and our accordion player, Remy, will be along soon. Grab your chair. You and Rascal need to be with friends tonight. We heard your man went to New Orleans for that all-fired, bigshot law enforcement meeting with the sheriff. Have you et?"

"I did; I had a slice of pizza." Wren folded her camping chair that was sitting next to the picnic table.

Desirada snorted. "I'll fix you a small bowl of hot gumbo to warm your soul. I've got something else for you too."

Desirada pulled out a medium-sized green velvet pouch with gold braids holding it closed. "This is for you, Wren. You'll know what to do with it." Desirada handed the pouch to Wren and dismissed it with a wave. "Put it away for now."

Wren dropped it into her backpack, and Desirada disappeared then returned with a huge covered bowl. She handed Wren a spoon. "Eat what you want, sha. I can put your leftovers in my refrigerator for later, or you can run it back to yours. We have a while before the music will get going."

Wren spooned up the hot gumbo. *I am burning my tongue, but I don't care. This is delicious.*

After she ate what she could, Wren leaned back and sighed. "That was so good."

"Run it back to your camper; I'll save your seat." Desirada cackled, and Wren and Rascal hurried back to the camper. After she put the gumbo in the refrigerator, she got a text.

She laughed when she saw Justin's selfie with an elevator. Wren squinted at a figure behind him then zoomed in.

"That's a woman; I can see her clearly, but I don't recognize her."

She replied, "I'm happy you have a sleek elevator."

"She's a beauty, but not a lot upstairs," Justin replied.

"That's hilarious. Forward the pic to Pat. There was a woman standing behind you; she looks like she's studying you."

"There's nobody there now, but I'll do it. Talk to you later."

Wren bit her lip. "Am I getting too paranoid, Rascal?"

Rascal trotted to the door; Wren shrugged, and they returned to the campfire.

After Wren sat in her camping chair, Rascal flopped down next to her.

"Did you hear about Simone?" Desirada whispered.

Wren nodded.

"We know more now. They assumed she was walking along the swamp and had a stroke; it looked like she had hit her head because she had a large lump on the back of her head, so the initial findings were she had fallen into the water and drowned.

On closer examination, they found a needle mark on the back of her neck and a lethal level of drugs in her body. An interesting bit of information is that when she was first reported missing, a deputy searched her house and didn't find any drugs, not even an aspirin. Later, the dispatcher received an anonymous call claiming there were drugs in Simone's house; after the same deputy returned, he found drugs in the oven and refrigerator, which were places he had searched previously. The state police are involved now."

"I'd heard they found drugs in her house, but nothing about a previous search before the tip."

"Interesting, isn't it? Here's another tidbit: there was a log on top of her body. Anybody walking by wouldn't have noticed, but an old coon dog stood by the water and bayed until his owner came to see what he'd found. What does that say to you, writer girl?"

"Simone's killer would have gotten away with it if it weren't for the old coon dog."

"That's right; in fact, if her body had been found even a day later, the authorities would have assumed the log drifted on top of her and wouldn't have found the needle mark. The bayou hides all sins."

"What about Penelope?" Wren asked.

"You are smart; Penelope disappeared the second she heard about Simone because she knows what her sister knew."

Wren gazed at Desirada. "What is that?"

"I don't know; only the killer knows."

Wren side-glanced at Desirada. *Yes, you do.*

The fiddler, Al, held up his hand for attention, and everyone became quiet. He pointed to the large pot on the tall, three-legged stool. "Tonight the gumbo pot's going to Miz Simone's family. Our hearts are broken that she's not here, but her spirit will always be in our hearts."

Al and Remy tossed in bills while the rest of the crowd gathered around the pot and added their offerings for the family. A tear slipped down Wren's face as she pulled out the emergency cash she had in her small jeans pocket and tossed it in.

After everyone was seated, the fiddler said, "Miz Simone would be a'haunting for the rest of our days if we don't make this a joyous gathering, so we're gonna kick this party off with some of our best tunes."

The fiddler and the accordion player broke into a song; Wren joined in with those sitting around the campfire who clapped to the beat.

After three songs, Remy said, "We're missing one of our most important members of our campfire gathering. Let's share our best Simone stories. I'll start."

"One second," a man said. He disappeared; when he returned, he set Simone's chair near the campfire.

The group cried and laughed at the stories, and Wren joined in with the tears and joy. During one particularly poignant story, Wren glanced at Simone's chair and blinked at the little girl in the tattered dress who stood behind the chair with her hands hovered like she had rested them on someone's shoulders. Tears streamed down the little girl's face, and Wren's tears overflowed.

Desirada patted Wren's hand. "You have a kind spirit, sha; we're glad you're here with us."

After the last story, the music started up, and the little girl disappeared. Wren stroked Rascal's back.

When the last song ended, Desirada said, "I'll walk back partway with you."

As they strolled toward Wren's trailer, Desirada said, "Some of us have suspicions about Lillith, but Simone must have had proof."

"Could Penelope have taken the proof with her?" Wren asked.

"You're thinking like me."

After Wren and Rascal went inside, Wren opened the velvet pouch Desirada had given her and smiled. "Rascal, Desirada gave us a mirror and a small music box with thirteen mismatched, broken earrings. I'll tape the mirror outside next to the door with strong tape and put out the box with the earrings near the steps. We're officially Cajun."

After Wren put out their Pere Malfait and rougarou traps, she took a shower and put on her pajamas.

When her phone rang, she was surprised. *Pat's calling me.*

"Wren, I've been trying to reach Justin, but he may have turned off his phone. He told me you said for him to send me the elevator photo. The woman in the background is Jake. If you talk to him before I do, let him know. What made you suspicious?"

"I don't know; it seems like lately everything puts me on edge."

"Sorry about that, but in this case, your instincts were spot on. I have an old friend on the New Orleans police force; I'm going to call him too."

After they hung up, Wren said, "The woman was Jake; she's stalking Justin. Pat's worried, and so am I. We should have gone with Justin and sneaked you into the hotel, Rascal."

Rascal yipped.

Wren stood at the window near the dining table and peered out. "I understand a little better now why Justin paces. I'm too anxious to write anything on the article right now, but I can look for any holes I'll want to plug." She lowered the window shades, pulled out her notes for the article, and checked her phone.

"Nothing from Gage yet. Maybe I'll hear from Babette, and I can ask her about her history paper. I'm convinced it will help me with the right theme for my article. I should have thought of it earlier; maybe Desirada could have contacted the Dupres."

Wren changed the sofa to her bed and stretched out with her notes. She didn't realize she'd fallen asleep until her phone rang.

*Good; it's Justin.*

"Hi, honey. I'm glad I came; the social was really interesting. I've been so isolated that I never thought anyone else had the same problems that I have in Hidden Gulch. There are three other guys who are rural sheriffs, two of them are from Louisiana, and the other one is from Texas; we're going to stay in touch."

"Did you look at your elevator selfie or hear from Pat?" Wren stretched as she sat up.

"No, I haven't; my phone has been off. I turned it on to call you."

"Look at it."

After a brief pause, Justin exhaled. "This is not good. I haven't seen Jake here, and I certainly didn't see her standing that close to me. She obviously didn't expect me to take a selfie in front of the elevator."

"Could it be possible she's attending the conference?"

"Not at all; it's a law enforcement management conference, not a general conference for law enforcement officers."

"Pat called me when he couldn't reach you; you should probably call him," Wren said.

"Okay, are you too tired for me to call you back after I talk to him?"

"Not at all." Wren fought off a yawn.

After they hung up, Wren indulged in a wide yawn, and Rascal copied her.

"I'd like a cup of hot tea. Do you want to go outside for a break?"

Rascal trotted to the door; when Wren opened the door, the air had a chill to it she didn't expect. She grabbed her jacket and on a whim, stuck her holstered pistol in a pocket. *I need to be more vigilant.*

When they stepped outside, the trees rustled in the light breeze. While Rascal investigated the area around the trailer, Wren listened as the trees whispered, "Mara, Mara." When a gust of wind whipped through Wren's hair, the trees moaned.

Rascal faced the restrooms and stood on point as he softly growled. Wren narrowed her eyes as a dark figure darted behind the building. She casually strolled to the camper; when she opened the door, Rascal jumped inside, and she followed him.

After she locked the door, she put a pot of water on the stove and turned on the burner. While she waited for the water to heat, she dropped a tea bag into her cup. "I don't know who that was, but I wouldn't have noticed them if you hadn't alerted."

When her phone rang, she exhaled. "Hi, honey. I guess you reached Pat."

"Sure did; he's going to make some calls tomorrow because we think this has to be a pattern of behavior for Jake, and she's somehow been able to slide under the radar. So, what did you do today?"

Wren told him about Naomi, the campfire, the stories about Simone, and what Desirada told her about Simone's death.

"What an evening; I'm sorry I missed the stories. It's a shock that Simone was murdered. I'm thinking it was a mistake for me to leave."

"When Pat told me the woman was Jake, I was mad at myself because I should have gone with you, and Rascal agreed we should have sneaked him in, so we could watch your back. I finally understand what you mean when you tell me you wish you could be here," Wren said.

"It's hard, isn't it? Change of subject: do we want to take our time returning to Arizona by taking four days to travel, or do we want to take three?" Justin asked.

"I'm ready to be in Hidden Gulch, so we can settle in, but it's over 1,400 miles from here; Traveling is too exhausting to spend more than seven or eight hours a day on the road. How many miles a day were you thinking?"

"If we go a little over four hundred miles a day, we could make it in three days; we can always map it out and make our first day on the road our longest," Justin said.

"We can't travel as fast as a car with the fifth wheel. So you're saying see how far we can reasonably go? I suppose we could, but don't you think one extra day on the road wouldn't be bad at all because we'll be together, and we can take our time?"

"I don't..."

Wren interrupted him. "I forgot to tell you about Babette's high school history project. She wrote a paper on the history of the campground. Naomi was going to see if Babette's mother still has her copy of it." Wren tried to stifle her yawn, but it got away from her. "If I had something like that for background, the article will be very easy for me to write."

"That's great." Justin exhaled. "You must be tired; I know I am. I'll call you in the morning. I love you, sweetheart."

After they hung up, Wren turned off the lights and curled up in her bed with Rascal on the floor next to her. She drifted off to sleep while the trees whispered, "Mara."

# Chapter Six

The next morning, Rascal nudged Wren's hand and whined. Wren stretched. "Time to get up already?" Wren threw on a jacket and her slippers before she stepped outside with Rascal into the predawn darkness.

While Rascal wandered around their campsite, Wren watched as two RVs slowly rumbled toward the exit.

After they went inside, Wren started the coffee maker; while she measured and poured Rascal's breakfast into his bowl, her phone rang.

When she answered, Justin asked, "Hi honey, how did you sleep?"

"I slept straight through the night with no nightmares; I had to make my own coffee this morning because I didn't remember to set it up last night, which was a bummer." Wren giggled. "That's a pretty wimpy complaint, isn't it? What about you?"

"I thought I was going to be awake most of the night worrying about you and what I needed to do about Jake, but I fell asleep and woke when my alarm went off. No coffee yet; I'll get some when I go downstairs."

"What's your agenda for the day?" Wren asked.

"My new group is meeting for breakfast. The panel I'm on is scheduled for nine o'clock; I'm really glad because I won't have to stew about it all day. What about you?"

"I'm going to see what I can do about following up on Babette's paper." Wren poured a cup of coffee. "I have my coffee; you need to get yours. I love you more than ever, honey."

"I love you, sweetheart. You know if I could hitch a ride back today, I would."

"Don't you dare."

"I won't, but I'll still wish I could. The guys and I are talking about doing our own thing for lunch."

"Enjoy your day."

After they hung up, Wren made up her bed and raised the shades. She poured a cup of coffee and sat at the dining table to watch the neighbors as they headed toward the exit.

"That's life at a campground, Rascal; except for the few perms, people come, and people go." She sighed. "I sound sappy, don't I? I'd be a terrible campground manager."

After she finished her second cup of coffee, Wren showered, dressed, and stuck her pistol into her inside waistband holster and her phone into her back pocket. "Let's take a walk and see if we can find Desirada."

They walked to the party tent and the fire ring that would have appeared abandoned except for the few chairs that remained.

Wren smiled. *Some people like to sit in the same place.*

A tear welled up when she saw Simone's chair was undisturbed. *They're not quite ready to tell her goodbye.*

Wren inhaled the aroma of the charcoal remains in the center of the ring. "I love the smell of an old campfire."

The young girl in the tattered dress appeared and cocked her head as she gazed at Wren.

"I'm looking for Desirada," Wren said.

When the ghostly waif walked away from them, Wren and Rascal followed her. The young girl stopped in front of a large, old single-wide trailer with its sides greenish brown from sitting so long in the shade. The young girl waved before she disappeared.

Rascal barked twice, and Desirada came to the door. "Come on in, you two; to what do I owe the visit?"

"We don't mean to bust in on you," Wren said.

"Don't be silly; come on in. I'll pour you some sweet tea; the only treat I have for Rascal is an animal cracker. Would that be okay?"

"I guess one would be okay," Wren said.

"Here's an elephant for you, Rascal."

Rascal sat politely then gently took the cookie from Desirada.

While Desirada filled two large glasses with ice and poured the tea, Wren glanced around the trailer. The floors and the kitchen countertops were gleaming; a large, old-style, console television was placed against a wall across from a three-cushion sofa. Two pillows with faded yellow pillow cases and a hand-crocheted blue shawl were on the sofa.

"I appreciate the traps you gave me," Wren said. "Rascal and I put them out last night."

"How did you sleep?" Desirada asked.

"Really well."

"Good, then nothing bothered you."

Desirada set the two glasses on her Formica-topped dining table, and the two of them sat.

"How can I help?"

"Naomi told me that Babette wrote a paper in high school that was the history of Cypress Knees Campground. It will help me a lot with the article I'm writing for the travel magazine."

"I don't know nothing about any school paper that Babette wrote, but I have a copy of Simone's article the newspaper published fifteen years ago for the Mahoneville Festival. It's the history of Mahoneville and the Cajuns who came from Arcadia in Canada, but about half of it talks about the campground. Babette was always a smart girl; maybe she used it as one of her sources for her paper. You can snap a picture with your phone if you like."

Desirada went to the back of her trailer and returned with a faded-brown newspaper inside a clear plastic storage bag. She slipped out the newspaper from the bag and carefully smoothed it out on the table.

"Wow, it was on the front page," Wren said.

"Yep, and it continues on page three."

Wren snapped a photo of the front page; after Desirada turned the page for her, she snapped pages two and three.

Desirada turned to the last page. "You might as well get the whole paper."

Wren took a picture of page four.

While they sipped their tea, Wren asked, "I heard somebody say something about a new Lilith. Do you know what that's about?"

"You see the little girl, Mara, don't you?"

Wren nodded.

"She's particular who sees her; do you know why you do?"

"Why?"

"She thinks you can stop Lilith; she'll help you."

"What do I need to know to stop Lilith?"

Desirada picked up their empty glasses and set them in the sink. "I made beignets earlier. Would you like to take a few home?"

*I'm being kicked out, but nicely.*

"I'd love it." Wren rose.

Desirada put four beignets in a small brown sack and smiled as she handed the sack to Wren.

"Thank you for the newspaper article." Wren carried the sack to the door where Rascal waited for her.

As Wren reached for the door handle, Desirada asked, "Journalists don't reveal their sources, do they?"

Wren glanced back before she opened the door. "Absolutely not."

On the way back to their camper, Wren shook her head. *Why doesn't Desirada want anyone to know she has the old newspaper article?*

Wren rewarmed the coffee then sat at the dining table with her coffee and the sack of beignets while she read the article Simone had written.

"This article is perfect; I can write my travel article with Simone's background and my campground observations. According to Simone's article, the moaning in the trees is to remind everyone of what Tante Julie Brown sacrificed to keep the people safe and that the cypress knees kept Pere Malfait from taking Mara away from the swamp when the hurricane swept everything else out to sea."

Wren grabbed another beignet and refilled her coffee. "Except I don't want to mention Mara, so I'll write the article, at least for now, with the trees mourning all those who were lost because the cypress knees couldn't save everyone."

When she took a big bite, powdered sugar dropped on her dark green shirt; after she set down her beignet to brush it off, she added the fine, white powder from her fingers to what was already on her.

She shrugged. "I'll change my shirt after I finish this beignet. These are scrumptious."

After she finished her breakfast, Wren washed her hands and changed her shirt before she sat down at the table; her fingers flew over the keys as the words tumbled out of her head and through her fingers as she furiously typed.

When she wrapped up the article, she exhaled and leaned back. "Not bad except for all the red and blue lines with notations of suggested corrections. I need more coffee before I can deal with the complaints of my editing software."

Wren closed her laptop and pushed it away from her before she emptied the last of the coffee into her cup and grabbed the last beignet. "I may have to do laundry today because it won't take the ants long to scout out my powdered sugar shirts."

Wren sat at the table and gazed out of the window while she sipped her now-cold coffee and dropped a cloud of powdered sugar on her shirt and her jeans. "The campground has emptied, Rascal, except for a few stragglers; maybe the article will convince guests to stay an extra day, which would be an easy way to increase their revenue, besides attracting campers with the mystery of the cypress knees."

Wren's eyes widened. "I came up with the perfect name for the article: 'The Mystery of the Cypress Knees.' What do you think, Rascal?"

Rascal grinned and trotted to the door.

Wren glanced down at her shirt and jeans. "Let me wash my hands and change clothes. Can you wait long enough for me to gather the laundry?"

Rascal flopped down in front of the door.

After Wren dressed and added towels and her pajamas to the laundry basket, she put the laundry detergent on top of the clothes.

"Ready?" Wren Rascal headed toward the laundry room. "Isn't it refreshing to be doing something that's normal, Rascal?"

Rascal yipped as he raced toward a taunting squirrel near the laundry building.

Wren glanced toward the registration building. *Naomi is already here.*

After Wren started the washer, she picked up a book on the table with a hand-printed sign that was taped to the cinderblock wall. "Take one, leave one."

As Wren looked through the books, she smiled. "Either fantasy stories were the most popular books thirty-five years ago, or that's what the campground readers like. That would be interesting to research, but this one looks like a classic to me." Wren sat on the lone, rickety, white plastic chair and read while Rascal sat near the door.

Rascal nudged her when the washer stopped. "I am totally lost in this book. It's fantasy, but it's absolutely hilarious."

Wren tore out an advertisement card for burial insurance that was inserted in the middle of a magazine; she stuck it into the book as a bookmark.

After she transferred the laundry to a dryer and put the coins into the slots, the coin slide wouldn't budge. Wren tossed the laundry into another dryer, put in the coins, and started the cycle. When Rascal growled a low growl, Wren joined him at the door and peeked out as a car crept past the laundry and toward the camping cabins row. After the car stopped at the first cabin, a woman with a floppy wide-brimmed straw hat stepped out of the driver's seat and glanced around before she pulled two overflowing shopping bags, a pillow with no pillowcase, and a backpack from the backseat and carried them into the cabin. She returned to her car and opened the trunk; after she removed a large suitcase, she closed the trunk and went inside her cabin.

"I don't remember ever seeing a lone woman rent a camping cabin, not that there's any reason she shouldn't; although I would have expected someone who was traveling to stop later in the day. She looked more like the hotel-type to me; what do you think?"

Rascal whined.

"We're too suspicious and overly nosy, aren't we?"

After Wren returned to her chair and opened her book, she said, "Maybe I'll go see Naomi after we take the clothes back to the trailer; are you going to stay outside?"

When Rascal barked, Wren nodded while she picked up her book.

Wren smiled as she read until Rascal bumped her book. "Is the dryer finished? Sorry, have you been trying to get my attention?"

She stuck the card into the book, dropped the book into her backpack, and shifted the clothes from the dryer to her basket., then she and Rascal went to the trailer.

After they returned, Wren dumped the clothes onto Justin's bed and stared at the pile. "I didn't think this out, Rascal. Do you think I should have asked Justin if it would be okay if I washed his things? I threw everything into the washer; what if he's more particular and separates his laundry by color or fabric? What if he likes his clothes folded a certain way? Do I let them get wrinkled? Would I be snooping if I put his clothes away? I can hang up his shirts, right?"

Wren exhaled. "I need to slow down; I dropped into panic mode and sounded like Betsy for a minute there, didn't I?"

While Wren sat on the edge of the bed, she sent a text to Justin. "I did laundry and included yours."

After a few deep breaths, Wren rose and quickly sorted the clothes and folded them. She hung up Justin's shirts and stacked the rest of his things on the top of the three-drawer chest next to the wardrobe. She returned the basket and laundry detergent to their places in the bathroom before she took her clothes to the living room and put them away.

Wren added the new title to her draft article and emailed it to Kendra. "I actually feel like I'm accomplishing worthwhile goals instead of completely spinning my wheels, Rascal. Before we go see Naomi, I want to check my website email, just in case."

Kendra replied immediately, "Good timing; I've turned over your blog to Gage."

After Wren logged onto her website email, she said, "There's nothing from Naomi. Are you going with me, Rascal, or would you rather stay here?"

Rascal stared at her and didn't move until Wren opened the door; he groaned as he rose then lumbered to the door with exaggerated pain in each step.

"You don't have to go if you'd rather stay," Wren said. "I know you don't like Naomi, so I'll be careful and won't be long; it's your choice."

Rascal returned to his rug and laid down.

As Wren walked toward the office, she raised her eyebrows when the young woman from the cabin came out of the office in a rush. Her floppy hat covered her face. *She must be in a hurry.*

When Wren went inside the office, Naomi smiled at her. "Nice to see a pleasant face, Wren. What can I do for you?"

"I dropped by to tell you the coin slide on one dryer doesn't seem to work."

"Which one?" Naomi whipped out her pad and a pen.

"The one closest to the door."

Naomi jotted down a note on her pad then wrote and underlined laundry above her note. She tapped her pad with her pen for emphasis. "Got it. What else can I do for you?"

Wren headed to the freezer case. "I thought I'd splurge and treat myself to ice cream."

"Did you happen to run into our newest guest? She's a young woman like you; she's staying in a cabin overnight. Her fiancé is going to join her tomorrow; they're going to New Orleans for a destination wedding. Isn't that romantic?" Naomi tittered. "I told her there's a twenty-four-hour waiting period in Louisiana for a license, but she said that wasn't a problem for them."

Wren furrowed her brow as she picked out an ice cream cone with peanuts and chocolate on top. "That is romantic."

As Wren paid for her ice cream, Naomi continued, "She told me he'd be here tomorrow with his trailer, and they'd turn in her rental car. I got a little confused because I didn't understand how they could have a destination wedding in a fancy downtown hotel if they're staying at a campground, but I realized they probably love camping, so that's the plan for their honeymoon. She did ask if there were any other single people here, and I laughed and explained all our guests are couples except for some of our permanent guests who are widowed." Naomi chuckled.

When Wren reached the door, Naomi said, "I almost forgot to tell you I should be getting a copy of Babette's history paper tomorrow. Her mother couldn't remember where she'd packed it away."

Wren smiled. "Thanks for letting me know."

After she was back at the trailer, she put her cone in the freezer. She peered at the plastic sack that she had moved to the bottom rack. "I don't remember what this is, Rascal." She pulled out the sack and looked inside. "Butter pecan ice cream! I wonder if it was supposed to be a surprise. I'll have to ask him."

Wren glanced at the clock. "Lunch time; I'll be free to read all afternoon."

While Wren's slice of pizza warmed up in the oven, her phone rang.

After she answered, Pat said, "Justin's phone has been off; have you talked to him today?"

"Early this morning before breakfast. He has a full schedule today."

"That's what I thought; let him know my buddy in New Orleans went to the hotel early this morning to question Jake, and she had already checked out. She asked the desk clerk about renting a car; the desk clerk recommended the rental service that's associated with the hotel, no surprise. When my buddy checked with the rental company, they rented her a car on a three-day contract with unlimited mileage."

"Do we know anything about the car? Make, model, color, or license number?"

"I'll find out; why?"

"A hunch."

"No, it's more than that, Wren. Tell me."

While Wren pulled out her extra-crispy slice of pizza with the blackened edges from the oven, she told Pat about the young woman with the oversized floppy hat who checked in at the campground.

"That's not good; I'll tell you what we have. Cody and I have been making calls this morning and asking very pointed questions. Cody learned, off the record, of course, that Jake became obsessed with another student when she was in training; the young man was intimidated and talked to the head instructor who was less than sympathetic and suggested the young man wasn't law enforcement material if he couldn't handle a woman. The young man didn't want the word to get around that he was afraid of an attractive woman who was pursuing him, so he dropped out. He moved to Texas and has resumed his law enforcement career there."

"When was this?"

"About a year ago. We found several other instances that involved men in authority who have kept quiet because they were afraid the story would be flipped around so that they were the stalkers, not Jake. Cody believes Jake killed a man because he refused her advances and threatened to charge her with stalking and harassment; after he told me about it, I made more calls that pointed to a cover up in the investigation. Cody and I have a call in an hour with an old friend of mine with the FBI. Jake is dirty, Wren, stay away from her. I'll call the parish sheriff."

"Pat, the parish sheriff is in New Orleans with Justin. Don't tell Justin today she's here; he should stay where he is to give you and the FBI a chance to develop a plan. I'm certain she's waiting for him, and if I can stay out of her way, she won't think of me."

"The sheriff would have left someone in charge; I'll call, and if there isn't a senior deputy, I'll be checking in."

Wren bit her lip. "Don't be surprised if you can't reach the senior deputy because there was a murder of a prominent local woman at the campground the night before last, so their department is pretty deep in the investigation along with the Louisiana State Police."

Wren jumped when she heard something slam on the other end of the phone. *Did Pat slam his hand on his desk?*

Pat exhaled. "Does Justin know about this?"

"He knows the woman died, but he doesn't know she was murdered."

"That's actually good; can you get someone to tell Jake the place is crawling with cops because of the murder?"

"That will be easy; what do you expect that to do?"

"Maybe keep her close to her cabin, so she won't decide to look for you. We need to buy enough time for the rest of us to come up with a plan to stop her; if she knows about the heavy law enforcement presence, she'll want to stay out of sight while she waits for Justin to show up tomorrow," Pat said.

"If you can get me the information about the car Jake rented, I can confirm whether the woman in the cabin is her."

"I'll get that you to as soon as I can."

After Pat hung up, Wren turned to her lukewarm slice of pizza, but her phone buzzed a text and interrupted her.

She smiled as she read the text from Justin.

"The conference is great; learning a lot. On my way to the next seminar. Love you."

Wren replied, "Good news. Love you too."

Wren bolted down her pizza before her phone could interrupt her again.

"Rascal, I'm going back to the office for another ice cream cone. Are you coming along?"

Rascal went to the door, and the two of them headed to the office. Rascal stayed outside while Wren went inside.

Naomi smiled. "Didn't expect to see you again so soon."

Wren strolled to the freezer case. "I decided I'd get another cone for dessert tonight; it was tasty."

"I'm glad you enjoyed it. You should feel very safe here; the young woman from the cabin was here only ten minutes ago, and I told her the same thing."

Wren pulled out an ice cream cone, closed the top of the freezer case, and strolled to the counter.

Naomi continued, "The state police are investigating the death of a local to determine the cause of death, so we have an extraordinarily strong police presence."

"That's really comforting, thank you." Wren paid for her ice cream and left.

Rascal whined and pointed toward the dog park before they reached the camper. Wren squinted as she scanned the dog park; she finally saw a lab puppy prancing with a large stick. "Give me long enough to put my ice cream in the freezer and grab your leash, then we can go to the park."

On the way to the park, the puppy saw Rascal and barked excitedly.

"What do you see, girl?" A middle-aged man asked.

When the man saw Rascal and Wren as they neared the park, he called out, "Will your dog be okay with a rambunctious puppy with no manners?"

Rascal yipped, and Wren smiled. "He'll be fine."

The puppy jumped up on Rascal and nipped at him. Rascal gave a low growl, and the man's face paled. When the puppy sat, the man exhaled.

Rascal yipped and raced to the other end of the park with the puppy behind him.

Wren smiled. "It looks like Rascal's in the mood to do a little training."

Wren rinsed then refilled the dog bowl with water before she joined the man who stood near the bench.

# Chapter Seven

Rascal ran the puppy back and forth across the park five or six times before he trotted to the dog bowl. After Rascal took a quick drink, he yipped, and the puppy scrambled for the bowl and drank her fill.

The man chuckled. "Her tiny belly is certainly full, isn't it?"

"She was smart; she waited for Rascal to tell her it was her turn, so she's very trainable."

"Could Rascal help me teach her to stay?"

"Sure. Call her to you, tell her to stay, and step back. When she moves to follow you, Rascal will yip, so repeat the command for her to stay. When she does, give her a minute, then tell her okay; after she comes to you, tell her she's a good girl. She's smart, so it won't take more than two or three times for her to catch on."

After the second time, the man said, "Stay" before he turned and walked away to the gate; the puppy watched him.

"Okay!" the man said. The puppy tumbled as she scrambled to join him.

The man chuckled as he fastened the leash onto the puppy's harness. "You two are fantastic dog and people trainers; I underestimated how smart she was." He chuckled as he knelt and rubbed the puppy's face. "Good girl; you must have thought I was a real knucklehead."

After he left, Rascal yipped as Desirada strolled to the gate. "I was on my way back from the dumpster when I saw Rascal at work, so I had to stop and watch. He's very talented, isn't he? How's your article?"

"I finished it and sent a draft to my editor for review; I appreciate the help."

"On my way to the dumpster, a young woman, who is staying in a cabin, asked me if I knew about the police investigation and was it true there were a lot of cops around? I told her, of course. Do you have any idea what I was talking about?"

Wren smiled and patted the bench. "Come sit a minute, and I'll fill you in."

After Desirada sat next to her, Wren told her about Jake, including what Pat had learned, and what Naomi had told Jake. "We're hoping the idea of the place crawling with cops will slow Jake down enough to buy Pat some time."

"You don't think she'll be scared away?" Desirada asked.

"She's too obsessed for that to be a possibility."

"Deranged would be my word." Desirada snorted. "Maybe she needs something else to think about; you know, a slight diversion."

"Diversion? I don't think it would be a good idea to alert her we're onto her."

"Don't you worry yourself about that at all, sha; just roll with it." Desirada cackled as she rose.

Wren watched as Desirada hobbled back to her trailer.

"What do you think she has in mind, Rascal?" Wren rubbed her temple before she opened the gate.

When Wren and Rascal returned to the trailer, she went inside and grabbed an ice cream cone and her book. After she sat in her recliner and put her feet up, Wren said, "I need a diversion, so I can roll with it."

After two hours, Wren's phone buzzed a text. "This is A. from the fishing hole. Call when you can."

Armand picked up immediately. "Thanks. Everything okay with you?"

*Other than two killers loose at the campground?*

"I'm fine; is there anything I can do for you?"

Armand exhaled. "I can't check on Mags to be sure she's okay. It's my fault; I should have set something up with her, but I was afraid it would be discovered..." Armand sighed. "What's done is done. I know it's a terrible thing to ask, but would you go to the Cranky Crawfish, buy something from the store, and wander over to the Mud Bug Outpost to see if she's okay?"

"Rascal and I can do that. How do I get back in touch with you, or are you going to call me later?"

"I'll call you later, but if you ever need me, text me and start your message with any type of fish, so I'll know it's you."

"Okay; we'll get moving because it will take us almost an hour to get there, won't it?"

Armand chuckled. "I forgot you aren't local, even if Justin is my cousin; I'll text you the directions that will get you there in thirty minutes."

"Can I tell her you sent me?"

"No, get yourself or Justin something at the Cranky Crawfish store and treat yourself to a beignet and a coffee at the Mud Bug Outpost before you head back. You can walk from the Cranky Crawfish to the Mud Bug; you'll see the trail."

*I don't think I could eat a fifth beignet.* "That'll work; I'll talk to you later."

"Ready for a road trip, Rascal? I know I am; let's go to the Cranky Crawfish Store and do some shopping. We'll walk to the Mud Bug Outpost for a treat."

After Armand sent the text with the directions, Wren pulled up her hair into a messy bun and put on her Cranky Crawfish ball cap. Wren grabbed her backpack and locked the trailer door. When they were in the truck, she lowered Rascal's windows partway, so he could enjoy the smells as they drove to the Cranky Crawfish.

"I don't think I'd ever get used to the edge of the water being so close to the road; there's absolutely no shoulder to speak of." Wren focused on the road ahead.

Thirty minutes later, Wren parked in front of the Cranky Crawfish. "Some of the shortcuts scared me, Rascal, because half the time I couldn't tell if there was a road or a swamp around the next curve, but we didn't get stuck or lost. Are you going to wait on the porch or in the truck?"

Rascal whined.

Wren glanced at the wrap-around porch with rocking chairs, picnic tables, and a life-sized, hand-carved, wooden black bear that was near the door.

"Okay." Wren raised the windows before she hopped out and opened the back door for Rascal. When they reached the porch, Rascal flopped down next to the bear and out of the main pathway; Wren went inside.

She strolled through the aisles of the store to find the perfect surprise present for Justin. *We already have matching ball caps.*

She stopped at the pullover sweatshirts with the cranky crawfish logo embroidered on the chest. Wren held up a sweatshirt. *They have a wide pocket across the front and a hood, and I can get him the same camo pattern as his ball cap.* She found a tall length in his size then looked for the same style of sweatshirt for herself. She found the sweatshirts that were her size and smiled. *Here's one that's the same color as my ball cap.* She examined a different sweatshirt that was the same color as Justin's. *No, that would be too cutesy.*

Wren stared at the wall of fancy dog treats. She read ingredients before she picked out two different treats. After she paid for her items, the cashier folded the sweatshirts and placed them and the packs of dog treats into a large brown paper sack with twisted paper handles and the cranky crawfish logo on the side.

When Wren went outside, Rascal joined her; she strolled the trail to the Mud Bug Outpost while he investigated the path and its surroundings.

Rascal waited on the porch while Wren went inside the Mud Bug; her eyes widened at the number of customers, and she was tempted to put her hands over her ears to muffle the noise.

"It's a surprise to see you, Miss Wren; what brought you here?" Mags asked.

Wren grinned and raised her sack. "And a decent cup of coffee."

"Oo-ee, girl; you done gone Cajun on us, haven't you? Sit at the counter, so I can see your sweet face, and I'll bring you your coffee and a piece of strawberry pie."

"I don't think..."

Mags disappeared; Wren sighed as she selected the stool that was the farthest from the front door.

When Mags brought Wren her coffee and a large slice of strawberry pie topped with a generous layer of freshly whipped cream, Wren groaned.

Mags patted her hand. "Eat what you want; I'll box up the rest for you. You can have dessert tonight and strawberries for breakfast tomorrow."

"Thank you." Wren smiled.

When she took her first bite, Wren closed her eyes. "Mmm."

She sipped her coffee then took one more bite.

Mags stopped at the counter with a coffee pot in her hand. "What do you think?"

"Absolutely delicious. I'm going to have to take you up on the box."

Mags set the coffee pot on the counter. She slipped the pie into the box she'd held behind her back and put the box into a sack. After she handed the box to Wren, Mags leaned close across the counter and whispered, "Tell Armand I'm fine. Is he okay?"

Wren stared at her then giggled. "You know it; thank you so much."

Mags beamed. "Your coffee and pie are my treat; I'll see you tomorrow evening."

When Wren went outside, she said, "Let's go; I'll give you your surprise when we get to the truck."

Wren and Rascal hurried along the trail to the truck. After Wren opened the back door, and Rascal hopped inside, she put her shopping bag on the passenger's seat then hurried around to the driver's seat. She pulled out a package of treats and gave Rascal one piece. After he ate it, he nudged her neck.

"You're welcome, Rascal."

As Wren drove back to the campground, she said, "Mags knew Armand sent me to check up on her. I was really shocked when she told me to tell him she was fine." Wren giggled. "It might have looked like a wasted trip, but we'll enjoy the sweatshirts."

Rascal licked his mouth.

"And you'll enjoy your treats," Wren added.

As Wren parked behind the fifth wheel where Justin had parked it, her phone buzzed a text.

After she was inside, she put the strawberry pie in the refrigerator, Rascal's treats in the cupboard, and the large shopping bag on Justin's bed before she checked the text.

"It's from Pat, Rascal. He sent me the rental car license number. We can go to the laundry and wash the new sweatshirts."

Wren replied, "Will check."

After she carefully removed the tags from the sweatshirts, she dropped them into the clothes basket. She glanced around the trailer. "I washed everything earlier today, but the sweatshirts are bulky enough to make a load."

She put the laundry detergent and the medicine bottle of quarters on top of the sweatshirts. She slung her backpack over her shoulder. "Let's go."

Rascal ran ahead and waited for her at the laundry. After Wren joined him, she went inside and started the washer. "Now for the tricky part."

Wren stepped outside the laundry until she was within sight of the car parked at the first cabin. She held up her phone and snapped a photo of the campground then focused on the cypress trees and snapped another. Wren turned her phone and zoomed in on the back of the car and took two snapshots before she turned her back to the cabin and snapped a last photo of the campground. She exhaled as she returned to the laundry room.

She checked the photos of the license plate. "Both of them are clear. The license numbers are the same as what Pat sent me." She sent the photos to Pat.

Wren sent a text to Armand. "Piranha is fine."

Her phone rang. Armand's phone.

When she answered, he said, "Thanks, Wren. You gave me my first smile today."

"She knew you sent me to check on her. She whispered, 'Tell Armand I'm okay; how is he?' I said, 'Only the best; thank you so much.'"

"If anyone had overheard you, they wouldn't have understood what you were talking about; thank you, Wren."

"I went into the Mud Bug with a large shopping bag from Cranky Crawfish and ordered coffee and walked out with my shopping bag and an enormous slice of strawberry pie."

Armand chuckled. "It's a dangerous place; thanks again."

"I'm happy to help; let me know if I can do anything else."

After Armand hung up, Wren said, "I should have brought my book, but I wanted to limit the amount of time I'm out in the open. I'll pick out another one. Rascal, would you guard the door and let me know if anyone is coming to the laundry? There's only one door, but I could always go in the restroom here and lock the door."

Wren opened the laundry room door and left it cracked when Rascal went outside and stretched out on the concrete walkway in the shade.

Wren heard a woman yelling. She pulled the plastic chair to the high, narrow window to see what the commotion was all about. When she stepped up onto the chair, it wobbled. *Please don't collapse, chair.* She clutched the window board for more stability.

Naomi was in the driver's seat of the golf cart with full trash sacks in the back. Jake was waving a brown object that was roughly the size of a cardboard toilet paper insert in Naomi's face and screaming at her incoherently.

When Naomi didn't respond, Jake threw the object on the ground and smashed it with her heel then clutched her chest and stormed to her cabin while she wailed.

*Drama much?* Wren raised her eyebrows.

Naomi climbed out of the golf cart, picked up the object, and said something.

*Did she say darn cats? I need an excuse to go to the office.*

When the washer stopped, Wren tossed the sweatshirts into the dryer and sat in the chair to read.

While she read, Rascal whispered a bark that sounded like "boof", then he softly growled.

"Is it Naomi, boy? Come, lay down on the other side of me, so you won't scare her."

When Naomi came into the laundry room with paper supplies in her arms, she gasped. "I'm sorry, Wren; I didn't expect to see anyone in here, and I was worried it was...someone else."

Wren smiled. "We're chilling while the dryer's running; I appreciate having books in here to read."

"It is nice, isn't it? I suggested it to Babette a year or two ago, and she liked the idea."

While Naomi put the spare rolls of toilet paper and paper towels into the storage closet, she said, "I'll never understand city folks. You probably haven't noticed because they would have stayed away from Rascal, but there is a small colony of feral cats that live in the swamp nearby. Of course, I've been feeding them." She chuckled. "They do find strange things in the swamp and sometimes leave presents, but today takes the cake. One of them must have found a voodoo doll and left it on the porch of the first cabin. It was hardly recognizable, but you would have thought they'd left a dead mouse for our delicate camper based on her reaction. Did you hear the screaming?"

"No, I didn't; the hum of the machines in here drowns out any outside noise."

"Her reaction was impressive; I'll give her that."

"Did you say a voodoo doll?"

"That's probably what it was at one time. It's more like a wet piece of old burlap with a few old rusty needles stuck into it, but it did have Xs for eyes and a straight line for a mouth stitched on it and a few strings that could have been hair at one time still attached to its head."

"What a present. I'm not sure I would have recognized it; is she Cajun, do you think?" Wren asked.

"I don't think so; her complaint was that someone stepped onto her porch and left something nasty, but she did add that she was too strong for stupid voodoo." Naomi shook her head. "She's obviously not playing with a full deck. I'll talk to her later after she's calmed down and offer her a full refund if she doesn't want to stay."

Naomi exhaled. "I rarely tolerate that type of disrespectful behavior, but she's lucky I'm the acting campground manager. Our sweet Babette would have put a curse on her."

Wren chuckled. *Not Babette. Me, maybe.*

Naomi quickly checked the paper supply in the restroom then left.

When the dryer stopped, Wren opened the door. "They're still a little damp; I'll run them again because they're too heavy to finish air drying in this humidity."

After she restarted the dryer, Wren settled down with her book, and Rascal resumed his position at the door.

When the dryer stopped, Wren returned her book to the book table and collected the dry, warm sweatshirts before she and Rascal hurried to the trailer.

After she folded Justin's sweatshirt, she put it into the Cranky Crawfish sack and set the sack on the counter, so it would be the first thing he saw when he came into the trailer.

She picked up her book on the way to her recliner.

After she had read for a while, her eyelids drooped, and she yawned. "The book is interesting, but I'm having trouble keeping my eyes open; I really don't need a nap today."

Wren glanced at the clock on the microwave. "It's almost time for supper; shall we check out our new neighbors first?"

Wren put on her new ball cap and sunglasses and picked up Rascal's leash before they went outside. Halfway down their row, she said, "I forgot my phone." She sighed as she glanced back at the trailer. "We won't be long."

Rascal turned back to the trailer; Wren trudged along behind. "I hate backtracking for no reason."

She went into the trailer and picked up her phone then joined Rascal outside. Before she slid it into her back pocket, it buzzed with a text. Wren read the text. "Fishing hole. Do you know how to get to Cranky Crawfish? I'm in trouble. B."

Wren immediately replied, "Yes."

"Park on the west side of the lot."

"On our way. 30 min."

"Ready for an evening ride, Rascal? I feel like getting away."

Wren grabbed her backpack and a bottle of water from the trailer, then opened the back door of her truck for Rascal. Before she closed the door, Wren frowned. *I forgot to lock the door.*

She hurried to lock the trailer door before she closed Rascal's door. Wren exhaled. *I need to slow down; I don't want to look frantic.*

She casually climbed into the driver's seat, glanced back at Rascal, and smiled before she started the truck. "This is me in my relaxed mode. What do you think?"

Rascal laid his chin on the back of her seat near her shoulder.

Wren smiled. "You look completely at ease; we don't have a care in the world."

Wren crept to the exit before she turned onto the road and accelerated until she was speeding well over the posted limit.

When she glanced back at Rascal, his eyes were narrowed as he stared at her. "Nobody else is on the road, Rascal, so quit judging me."

Wren turned at the entrance to the Cranky Crawfish. After she parked on the west side of the lot, her phone buzzed a text.

Wren read the text from Babette. "Let Rascal out of the truck for a break, but don't close the door so I can hop in. Put Rascal back in and go inside and look around; maybe buy something."

Wren opened the back door, and Rascal hopped out. They stepped away from the truck and closer to the edge of the parking lot. Rascal marked a tree then they returned to the truck. When Rascal saw Babette lying on the floorboard, he hopped inside.

"I won't be long, Rascal; I need to find something for Betsy and Socorro."

Wren went inside and bought two sets of Cranky Crawfish hand towels and oven mitts. After she returned to her truck, she put her package on the passenger's seat before she backed out and headed down the driveway to the road. She wrinkled her nose and coughed. *The truck smells like a swamp.*

"Do I go back to the campground?" she asked.

"I don't know; I need to hide. If I could get to the campground, maybe Armand could take me to the fishing hole tonight, but I'm not sure that's what I want to do."

"You can hide in my trailer while we figure out what's best for you; what happened?" Wren asked.

"When I walked out of my house to go to work, someone was hiding behind my car, so I snapped my fingers and went back inside like I'd forgotten something. After I changed my shoes to swamp boots and threw my purse, shoes, and a jacket into a backpack, I slipped out the back door. I took my time as I hiked through the swamp so I could hear whether anyone had followed me. If they did, they were too far behind me to catch up. Armand knows you were coming to pick me up."

"There's a bottle of water on the back seat; did you find it?"

"No, but I've got it now; thank you."

"Why was someone hiding by your car?"

"I don't know who Lilith is, but she must think I do. Tante Simone told me she had ways to expose Lilith, but I didn't understand that's what she was saying until after she died."

Babette gulped down some water. "Tante Simone always called Lilith 'it', and I thought Tante Simone had no respect for Lilith, but now I'm not positive that Lilith is a woman, so I believe anyone could be Lilith or under her control except for you, Armand, Mags, and me."

Wren's eyes widened. *We switched from a difficult and dangerous situation to an impossible one with the only outcome being failure.*

"That's not good," Wren said.

After Babette finished the bottle of water, she exhaled. "Thanks for the water, Wren. I was parched even though I was surrounded by water. The day before Tante Simone died, she told me that if anything happened to her, she had some things for me in a box in her backyard, and if I ever couldn't find her, to look for the box."

Babette chuckled. "I was instantly transported back to the days when I was a child and spent part of my summers with Tante Simone, and we played a game. She would hide treats in a box in her backyard, and I would search for the box. Sometimes it took me all day to find the box, but that was mostly because I'd be distracted by butterflies, listening to the birds, or finding interesting rocks."

"What a great way to spend the summer," Wren said.

"If she hid a box for me in the backyard, it's well-hidden; no one could find it except me because I know all her favorite hiding places."

"Are you planning to look for the box?" Wren asked.

"I have to expose Lilith as quickly as I can to stop the extortion and before she kills someone else; the only thing I have is the box."

Wren nodded. "I'll help however I can. We can talk about it while we eat. I have enough leftover gumbo for both of us and strawberry pie for dessert."

Babette giggled. "I know where the strawberry pie came from; where'd you get gumbo?"

"Desirada gave me a covered serving bowl of gumbo yesterday."

"Enough for several meals, I'm sure."

As Wren turned at the campground, she said, "The best way I can think for you to get out of the truck without being seen is if I drive on the other side of the registration office, so you can hop out then come to my trailer. I'll have the trailer lights off, the shades lowered, and the door open, so you can come right in. Do you have any other ideas?"

"Drive to the dumpsters and stop a second; I'll hop out. It's closer to your trailer, and the security light there is burned out."

"The interior light of the truck automatically comes on when a door opens," Wren said.

"Your idea is better," Babette said.

When Wren stopped behind the registration office, Babette climbed out; Wren continued to her trailer.

After Wren went inside and pulled down all the shades, she joined Rascal who had remained on watch outside. When Babette dashed for the door and went inside, Rascal followed her. Wren briefly stood in the doorway as she scanned the campground then closed the door.

# Chapter Eight

"I can turn on the lights because no one can see inside, but they can see the lights are on, which makes everything normal. Do you want to take a shower? Do you have any spare clothes in your backpack?"

"No, but I do keep a change of clothes in the office. I'll go get them."

"Wouldn't it be better if I did?"

Babette narrowed her eyes. "Why would a guest have keys to the office?"

"Maybe I'm the camp host and after hours manager; who would know?"

"All the perms, but they wouldn't think anything of it." Babette sighed. "Okay; here are the keys, and my clothes are in a grocery sack in the storage closet."

"I'll lock the door when we leave, so you can take a shower while we're gone, or you can wait until we get back, if you like."

"I'm itchy, but I'll wait until you and Rascal return before I shower. Do you have a plastic bag I can use for my swamp clothes?"

After Wren put a plastic sack on the counter, Babette handed her campground keys to Wren. "This one is the key to the office, and this one is the key to the storage closet."

After Wren and Rascal went outside, Wren locked the door. As she hurried toward the office, she glanced back at the trailer and exhaled in relief. *I was right; the only lights showing are from the bathroom skylight and a leak around the large window shade next to the dining table.*

When Wren and Rascal reached the office, she unlocked the door then locked it behind her. "Do I turn on the lights?"

Wren went to the restroom, turned on the light, and left the door open. "That's not as much of an announcement that the office is open."

After she unlocked the storage room, she found the plastic grocery bag on the second to the top shelf and pulled it down. On her way out of the storage room, she saw a ring on the floor with a large pearl-like gem, picked it up, and stuck it into her jeans pocket.

She locked the storage room and turned off the restroom light then stood near the front door and waited in the dark for a few minutes. After she locked the office, Rascal trotted to the trailer, and Wren casually strolled along behind him.

She unlocked the trailer door. "We're home, Rascal."

When they went inside, Babette peeked out of the bathroom where she had been hiding. "I'm glad you said something, so I wouldn't freak out."

Wren handed Babette her clean clothes. "Here you go."

"Thank you; it will be nice not to be stinky."

"Did you find what you needed for your shower?"

"Sure did," Babette said. "I left the plastic bag with my wet clothes next to the door."

"I'll put your wet things in the back of my truck for now."

When Wren returned to the trailer, Babette was in the shower. Wren fed Rascal before she poured the gumbo into a pot. While the gumbo bubbled, Wren set the table for two with placemats, spoons, and paper napkins. Wren lowered the burner flame and stirred the gumbo when she heard Babette turn off the water.

When Babette came out of the bathroom dressed in clean clothes, she was towel drying her hair. "I may have a brush or a comb in my backpack, but I honestly don't care; I'm clean and didn't find any leeches, so that's all that matters."

Wren shuddered. *I didn't think about leeches in the swamp.*

"Would you like water, sweet tea, or wine to drink?" Wren asked.

"Sweet tea is obligatory with gumbo, isn't it?"

"Absolutely." Wren smiled as she pointed to the table. "Have a seat, and I'll pour the tea and dish up the gumbo."

While they ate, Babette said, "This is delicious."

"Do you care for anymore?" Wren asked after they had cleaned their bowls.

"Not at all; didn't you say something about strawberry pie?"

Wren put the leftover gumbo back into the refrigerator and pulled out the slice of strawberry pie then cut it in half.

"Where are the forks?" Babette asked.

Wren pointed to a drawer.

Babette put the forks on the table while Wren set down the small dessert plates.

Babette cut a small piece of pie with her fork. "I'm not sure I can eat all this, but I'll give it my level best."

Wren took a bite. "Mmmm. Me too."

When Wren heard the twang of the fiddle being tuned, her eyes widened. "Oh no, I can't go with you to Simone's house until late tonight. I can't miss the fire pit because I've gone every night I've been here."

"This might work out even better because if anyone thought I might have called you, being at the fire pit completely removes you from suspicion and makes it safer for both of us."

Wren slowly nodded. "No one would think you were at the campground, either."

"Is it unusual for you to get a text while you're there?"

"I don't remember getting one, but Justin did."

"Good enough; I can keep you posted by text. If you have to come rescue me, I'm completely confident you'll think up a wonderful excuse for having to jump up and leave."

"What about transportation? Do I need to take you somewhere and then pick you up?"

Babette shook her head while she searched through her backpack. "Here it is; I was looking for my knife. I'll walk to Tante Simone's through the swamp, which is actually faster than you could drive to her house."

She stuck the sheath with its knife inside her belt. She put on her jacket, slid her phone into the jacket's inside pocket, and slipped on the backpack. "I'm ready; what's the plan?"

Wren stuck her phone in her back pocket before she put on her jacket and picked up her backpack. "I'll turn off the lights, and Rascal will go out first. He'll warn us if anyone is near. If no one's around, you go outside, and I'll follow you. I'll leave the door unlocked, so you can go inside if you're back before I am."

"You aren't worried about leaving the trailer unlocked?"

"Rascal will know if anyone approaches the trailer and be happy to greet any potential intruders."

Babette rubbed Rascal's face. "You're a good boy," she cooed.

Rascal groaned and leaned against Babette's leg.

Wren turned out the lights. "Ready, Rascal?"

She opened the door, and Rascal hopped out.

"Go," Wren whispered.

Babette quietly went down the steps and disappeared into the dark.

After she went outside and closed the trailer door, Wren gazed at the overcast sky. *I hope she has enough light to see; it's darker in the swamp than it is here.*

Wren picked up her camping chair and caught up with Rascal who had dashed ahead to wait for her near the fire pit with Desirada.

"How was your day, sha?" Desirada asked.

Wren set her chair next to Desirada's. "I finished my blog and sent it to my editor, but most importantly, thanks to the newspaper article, I completed my Cypress Knees Campground article and sent it to the editor too."

Desirada peered at Wren. "I forgot to tell you that you'd enjoy reading the entire newspaper, didn't I?"

"I might have forgotten, but I'll do that."

The fiddler played a sweet, forlorn tune while the accordion player unpacked his instrument.

"Let's have a little fun here." Al switched to an upbeat song, and the folks around the campfire cheered as Remy joined him.

"I'll be right back." Desirada patted Wren's hand; she and Rascal disappeared.

When the music shifted to a familiar two-step song, all the couples jumped up and danced around the fire. Wren joined in with the laughter and clapped along with the music. At the end, the crowd applauded, and a few brave souls who had left their campers clapped too.

Desirada and Rascal returned. "Thanks for saving my seat." Desirada cackled.

The fiddler hollered as he motioned for the newcomers to come closer, "Grab yerself one of your camping chairs and come join us."

Several couples and a family with three children took him up on the offer and made a second row behind the campfire people.

Al held up his hand. When everyone quieted down, he pointed to the large pot that sat on a tall, three-legged stool. "Just like we say every night, this here's our gumbo pot for those who are moved to toss in a tip, but it ain't a requirement as long as you are enjoying our tunes." A few of the regulars dropped in tips, and three campers followed their example.

When the music started up again, Wren smiled as a few more campers placed chairs alongside the others.

"It's story time," Remy said as they ended a song.

"I've got a story," an elderly man who sat in a wheelchair said as he peered at the new arrivals. "Have you heard the story of the cranky crawfish?"

The campers shook their heads; one small boy spoke up. "No!"

The elderly man chuckled. "Well, boy, you're about to hear the strangest story you've ever heard; come closer."

The young boy gazed at his dad. When they picked up their camping chairs, the folks sitting closest to the old man shifted to make room. The boy and his dad carried their chairs to the space that had been cleared for them near the fire and the storyteller, while newly arrived campers moved into the now-vacated spots.

Rascal softly growled; Wren furrowed her brow and whispered, "What's wrong, boy?"

Desirada leaned down and scratched Rascal's ear as she cooed quietly, "I gotcha, boy; we'll be on guard."

Desirada shifted her chair slightly to an angle, and Rascal moved closer to her.

The elderly man cleared his throat; when he spoke, his Cajun accent had thickened. "Everybody knows if you want to see if there are any crawfish in a crick, you stick your big ole toe into the water, and Mister Crawfish will latch onto that toe quicker than a dog will snatch up a piece of andouille sausage that landed on the flo'."

The boy side-glanced at his dad, and his dad nodded; the boy leaned forward.

Wren smiled. *Our boy is hooked.*

"Now, crawfish ain't always been like dat. No sireee..."

While the old man spun his tale, Wren peeked at her phone. *Nothing.*

She scanned the attentive expressions on the faces of the people around the fire. *Everyone is enthralled with the story.*

Wren turned slightly to glance at the group of campers seated around her. *The entire campground is here.* Her skin crawled at the sight of Jake, minus her floppy hat, lingering in the shadows behind the seated campers.

Wren glanced at Desirada, who nodded and smiled. *Rascal had alerted to Jake, so Desirada had already spotted her.*

Wren exhaled. *I still have on my ball cap and my back is to her; Desirada moved her chair to more of an angle to keep an eye on Jake.*

When the storyteller ended his tale, everyone laughed and applauded. After the crowd settled down, the elderly man asked in a quiet voice, "You going to be here Saturday, boy?"

The boy turned to his father with pleading in his voice, "Are we, Dad?"

Those who were close enough to hear murmured, "Aww," and "Say yes, Dad."

The boy's dad smiled. "We sure will."

"Good choice, Dad." The fiddler saluted the man with his bow. "We'll be back with more music and stories on Saturday; meanwhile, we got a few more tunes tonight, and don't forget the gumbo pot. If'n you can't stand to sit still, feel free to dance."

A man behind Wren tapped her on the shoulder and whispered, "Gumbo pot?"

Wren pointed. "It's their tip jar."

"Thanks."

Wren smiled as the man whispered to his neighbor, "The gumbo pot is their tip jar."

*It will get around; campers are generous and love listening to authentic local music.*

"If standin' ain't your best skill, raise them arms and clap your hands," Remy added.

Al tapped his toe three times, and then the air was filled with music.

Wren swayed to the music, smiled at the others around the fire, and occasionally glanced over her shoulder.

*Jake's still there glaring at the crowd. I hope her eyes burn. Ooo; that was mean. Glad I didn't say it out loud.*

Wren glanced at Desirada, who laughed.

Wren rolled her eyes. *I wouldn't be a bit surprised if she read my mind.*

During the next song, Desirada leaned close to Wren and said, "She's gone; we're boring."

Wren raised her arms, did jazz hands, and bobbed her head in her version of dancing while sitting; Desirada cackled.

When the song ended, Al said, "This is our last song; we'd love to send you off with a sweet melody for a restful night, but that's not our style. We're going to send you out into the night with your blood pumping. Stand if you can and stomp to the music or clap while you sit and fasten them seat belts, mama, 'cause we're gonna rattle your teeth and shake your soul."

The accordion player said, "Now you've gone couyon for sure; let's hit it."

They immediately went into a tune that sounded so rowdy it would have been risqué if it had words. The crowd danced, stomped, and clapped to the music.

At the end of the song, the campers whistled, clapped, and cheered as the musicians packed up their instruments. The crowd filed past the gumbo pot before they picked up their chairs and headed toward their campers. On their way, the night was filled with excited conversations about the evening of stories and music.

"I briefly mentioned the music and the campfire in my article, but after tonight, should I say something more? Is the music pretty regular?"

"Why don't you talk to that fiddler man and ask him?" Desirada said.

When Wren approached Al, he smiled. "Hello, Miss Wren, what can I do for you?"

She returned his smile. "I'm writing an article about the campground for a travel magazine, and I wondered if I can mention the music and stories as part of the charm of the campground?"

He stared at her. "You'd do that?"

"If you don't mind; y'all are providing a remarkably unique entertainment. People rarely spend any time at all outside even when they're camping and would never have dreamed they could enjoy a relaxed evening around a campfire and an hour or two of fun with their families and other campers that were no longer strangers after they shared such a wonderful evening of music, stories, and laughs."

Remy elbowed Al. "Tell her yes."

Al grinned. "We appreciate you."

Wren smiled. "Then it's done."

The men held out their hands, and Wren shook hands with them before she joined Desirada and Rascal.

"What's couyon?" Wren asked while she picked up her chair.

"It's wildly foolish or nonsensical; it's usually only said as a joke, like tonight," Desirada said. "What did they say?"

Wren rolled her eyes. "I know you heard every word."

"I was being social; what did they say?" Desirada asked as she walked with Wren and Rascal toward the fifth wheel.

"They said, yes."

"See? You can be social too. I was afraid they'd be too prideful. They're talented musicians, but around here, that don't hardly pay the bills. I understand Remy sends almost all his money to an assisted living facility in Texas for his uncle. Al has a wife and family and is a hard worker, but he doesn't have extra funds for what most folks consider necessities like regular dental and medical checkups; generous tips will help them take care of their families like they want."

As Desirada turned to go back to her trailer, Wren said, "Thank you, Desirada; I'm thrilled to be included in your master plans."

"Good." Desirada disappeared into the night.

Before they reached the trailer, Wren stopped to send a text to Kendra. "I have an addition to the article. Will send it tomorrow."

"Rascal, let Babette know we're here," Wren said when they reached the door.

After Rascal yipped, Wren opened the door. When they went inside, Wren closed the door and reached for the light switch.

Babette said, "Don't turn on the overhead lights."

She turned on the light over the stove. "My eyes are used to the dark; the sudden bright light would have been too shocking."

"Could you hear the music?" Wren rinsed then refilled Rascal's water bowl.

"Yes, and it was amazing; I'm embarrassed to say I didn't know it was a regular thing because I'm not here at night."

"I talked to the musicians; they've been playing almost every night for a while and plan to continue. I'm adding them to the travel article because they are a truly unique addition to a campground."

"You are? I would never have thought..." Babette's voice cracked. "Thank you; shouldn't I pay them?"

"Does the campground business have medical or dental insurance for staff?"

"I'm pretty sure we do, but I'll check on that; would that help them?"

"Probably, but you'll figure all that out." Wren snickered. "If you ask Desirada for help, she'll tell you exactly what to do."

"I can do that. I couldn't hear the story; how was it?"

"It was genius; I think the storyteller made it up on the spot."

"Did you record it?"

"No; it didn't seem right because I didn't have his permission. Did you find what you were looking for? Do you want some sweet tea?"

"Tea sounds good." Babette turned on the light over the dining table. "There, that's not too bright. I found a box in a resealable plastic bag, but it was empty."

Wren poured their tea. "Oh, no; do you think Lilith got to it before you did?"

"I did at first, and I was really upset, but I realized Lilith wouldn't have bothered to rebury the empty box, much less in a plastic bag, so I carefully put it in the same spot. Simone must have left the empty box for Lilith. The longer I was there, the more spooked I became because I imagined Lilith was standing at the edge of the trees watching me, so I pretty much bolted."

"What's next?" Wren sat with Babette at the table and sipped her tea.

"On my way back, I realized Tante Simone told me last week that my yard had much better hiding places than her yard because no digging was necessary. I have a couple of ideas; do you think you could drop me off close to my house early tomorrow morning?"

"I could do that." Wren said.

When Babette set down her tea glass to cover her mouth when she yawned, Wren said, "I'll pull out my bed; you can sleep there, and I'll sleep in Justin's bed, but you can't tell him."

Babette smiled. "I don't need to take your bed; I'll be perfectly comfortable sleeping in a recliner." She yawned again. "It's been an emotionally and physically exhausting day."

"Don't be silly." Wren unfolded the sofa into a bed and added sheets, a blanket, and a pillow. "There; that's yours."

Wren's phone rang. "It's Justin; I'll take Rascal outside for a few minutes; when I come in, I'll go to the bedroom while I talk to him."

Wren answered as she opened the door for Rascal. "Hi, honey. Rascal and I are going outside for his last break of the night. How was your day?"

"This conference has been amazing for me; Pat's been after me for ages to take some classes, but we never considered a professional development conference. My buddies and I think we need to attend a conference every year. We're talking about the one in Texas next year. What do you think?"

"Makes sense to me," Wren said. "Rascal and I will be fine by ourselves in Hidden Gulch."

Her eyes widened as Justin continued talking. *Why did I announce I'll be in Hidden Gulch next year? Did Justin politely ignore it?*

Rascal wandered around their campsite; Justin continued as he talked about the speakers, their topics, and the people he met.

When Rascal nosed the stairs, they went inside; Wren locked the door behind them and glanced at the easy rise and fall of the form wrapped in a blanket on her bed. *Babette's already asleep.*

Wren turned off the lights in the living area then turned on the light in the bedroom before she sat on the edge of the bed while Justin continued to talk. After Rascal flopped on the rug near the front door, Wren closed the bedroom door.

"That's pretty much my day; what about you?" Justin asked.

Wren told him about Babette, Desirada, the music, the story, the campers, and the addition to her article.

"I'm becoming immune to your typical days; you didn't get hurt, and nobody shot at you, so I'm happy, but you didn't mention Jake," Justin said.

"I can't believe I left out the best part of my day." Wren giggled and told him about the voodoo doll.

Justin chuckled. "That's priceless; Desirada is definitely in your corner. What's the plan for tomorrow other than I'll be there in the afternoon?"

"Babette wants to check the yard at her house, so I'll drop her off. After I revise the article for the Cypress Knees Campground, I might do laundry."

"I'll bet you're tired," Justin said.

Wren yawned. "I wasn't until you mentioned it. What's your schedule tomorrow."

"Breakfast with the guys, then the rest of the morning is a debriefing. After the luncheon, Vic and I will head back."

"I can't wait to see you. Are we going to leave Saturday or Sunday?"

"I haven't thought about it. What do you want to do?"

"Sunday makes sense; it gives you a day off before a long day of driving."

"I'll be..." Justin yawned. "Sorry; I'll be fine."

Wren smiled. "I love you, honey; I'll see you tomorrow."

"Sweetest words I could possibly hear; I love you too."

After Wren climbed into bed, she inhaled his pillow. *Smells like Justin.* She sighed as she hugged the pillow and closed her eyes.

She immediately sat up. *I'm supposed to read the newspaper.* Wren propped up the pillow behind her then pulled up the newspaper pages on her phone. After she'd read the four pages, she furrowed her brow. *Not much to read. The article Simone wrote was most of it except for a few classifieds and the obituaries.*

Wren read the pages more slowly and frowned as she read the classifieds. *The legal section lists Coastal Landsavers Investment, Inc. as the purchaser of five foreclosed properties in the area. I wonder if that's what Desirada wanted me to see?*

After she fluffed her pillow, Wren set her phone on the small shelf next to the bed and closed her eyes.

Wren woke to a man coughing outside the fifth wheel near the bedroom window, and Rascal whined. *It's still dark; what time is it?*

She raised on her elbow, peered at her phone, and blinked in disbelief. *It's three o'clock in the morning, y'all.*

"I don't care what you were told; she didn't come to the campground," a man grumbled. "She wasn't in the office, restrooms, or either of the two empty cabins."

His dry, hacking cough interrupted him before he continued, "She would have gone to her brother's; we're wasting our time here."

Wren pulled away the blind from the window, but she couldn't see the men. *They must be right under my window.*

"Yeah, well, you tell her that," the second man's voice was squeaky and grating. "She already told us she checked the brother's place herself. I'm not crossing her. If she wants me to walk around in the dark at the campground, I'll walk around in the dark in the campground; you can do whatever you want."

"I'm not complaining," the first man raised his voice, then was racked with a fit of coughing before he choked out the words, "Don't you go telling her I was complaining."

"Do you want to wake the entire campground?" the man with the squeaky voice hissed. "That coughing is bad enough; you need to get cough drops. I'm getting outta here before you get every dog in the campground barking."

Rascal growled.

"See, told you." The pitch of the man's squeaky voice was even higher.

Wren watched as two men raced to a car. After the engine started, the driver turned on the headlights and spun out in his rush to get away.

Wren climbed into bed. *They were looking for Babette.*

Wren lay awake as she listened for anyone else approaching the fifth wheel.

# Chapter Nine

The camper was dark when Wren woke; she opened one eye to peer at her phone. *Five o'clock. I don't want to wake Rascal or Babette.* She yawned and rolled onto her side but couldn't stop thinking about what the men had said. *Whoever she is, she checked the brother's place herself. I need to check with Armand.*

Wren sent a text to Armand. "Circling hammerheads. Text me when you have time."

Armand responded immediately. "Is all okay?"

*I hope I didn't wake him.* "We're fine. Can I call you?"

Wren put her phone on silent and closed the bedroom door as her phone flashed.

"What's up?" Armand asked when she answered.

Wren pulled the bed covers over her head and whispered, "Two men were outside of my trailer at three o'clock this morning. From what I heard, a woman sent them to the campground to look for Babette. One man said the woman had already checked with you, and Babette was not at your house. Who could that be?"

"Nobody's asked me about Babette; I'll check with my wife later, but she would have told me if anyone was asking about my sister. Is Babette okay?"

"She's fine; she took a shower last night, and I picked up her clothes for her from the office."

"You did? Wren, take them back. Have her wrap up in a blanket or something, but her clothes can't be missing from the office. Do it now; call me back, so we can talk."

After they hung up, Wren opened the bedroom door and exhaled in relief because the light was on over the stove.

"Good morning, Babette. I talked to Armand, and he told me I have to take your clothes back to the office. Wrap up in a blanket, and I'll take your dirty clothes with me and drop them off at the washer."

"That's crazy, but we'll find out why later, won't we?"

Babette grabbed the blanket from the bed and the sack from the counter and rushed to the bathroom.

"Here you are," Babette said. "The keys are on the counter."

Wren grabbed the laundry detergent and hurried out with Rascal on her heels. She grabbed both sacks of still-wet, stinky clothes out of the truck bed and rushed to the office. Wren unlocked the door, then used the light on her phone to unlock the storage room.

After she replaced the sack on the shelf where she had found it, Wren locked the storage room then the office, and hurried to the laundry room. When they went inside, she tossed the clothes into the washer; while she put in the coins, she said, "Have you noticed our latest hobby is hanging out in the laundry room, Rascal?"

She waited until the washer started before she rushed back to the fifth wheel with the detergent bottle. When Wren and Rascal went into the trailer, she inhaled the welcome aroma of coffee.

Babette poured two cups of coffee and smiled. "It was the least I could do since my brother has obviously lost his mind. No one knows about my spare clothes except family. I've always had them there."

After Wren gave Rascal his breakfast, she sat with Babette at the table. "What about security cameras?"

Babette sipped her coffee and frowned. "There aren't any. Actually, anyone who is local would know I would have a change, because that's what everyone does. Naomi keeps her change of clothes in a bottom drawer that we don't use for anything else near the register."

"Armand's waiting for me to call him back." Wren picked up her phone.

When Armand answered, Wren said, "I put Babette's clothes back and threw her swamp clothes into the washer; they'll be dry before daybreak. Babette made coffee while I was gone."

"Put me on speakerphone."

"Okay," Wren said.

Armand continued, "I have a better idea of what might be going on. Lilith has been making loans for years to tide people over until payday. It's not a habit that any of our family got into, which is why we weren't aware that it went from a service to a burden. The problem is that if you didn't make your payment on time, you'd be charged a fee. The fee hasn't been too bad until a year ago when Lilith jacked up the fees."

"Like how?" Babette asked.

"Say you took out a hundred-dollar loan with a twenty-dollar week payment each week for ten weeks, and your payment was due every Wednesday at two o'clock."

"So, you'd borrow a hundred and pay back two hundred over two and a half months," Babette said.

"Right, however, about a year ago, the late fee policy, as Lilith called it, was implemented. If you got stuck at work or in traffic and missed the two o'clock payment, you'd be assessed a ten dollar late fee the first time, and your payment would go up five dollars. If you have a second missed payment on your new twenty-five dollar payment, the fee is fifteen dollars, and your new payment becomes forty dollars."

"For the remaining ten weeks?" Wren asked.

"That's what you might think, but it turned into a sliding scale. Lilith had some convoluted formula that extended the time before the debt would be satisfied."

"That's why so many people are taking on second and third jobs," Babette said.

"With all this extra money she has from her compounding interest loan scheme, Lilith has hired some goons that she calls agents. The agents collect the money owed to Lilith and tack on a little protection fee of their own. People are walking away from their homes; their property is going into foreclosure, and an investment group is buying up the parish property by property."

"Does the sheriff know about this?"

"He's been trying to get a handle on it for a while, but nobody's talking. I think Simone got her hands on some damaging records as far as Lilith is concerned and maybe even lifted some money and returned it to folks."

"How could Simone do that? She was brilliant, but she was elderly and fragile," Wren said.

"True, but while Lilith had her thugs, Simone had her posse," Armand said. "There's been a war going on for a while, but Lilith made a mistake when she killed Simone; she must have thought the posse would disband with Simone gone, and her troubles would be over. The posse has doubled down and joined forces with the official posse."

Wren exhaled. "Are you part of Simone's posse, or are you more official?"

Armand chuckled. "I'm a good guy; does that help?"

Babette rolled her eyes.

"Yes, so what do you need for me to do?" Wren asked.

"You're not posse, Wren; you're off the hook," Armand said.

Wren side-glanced at Babette, who winked.

"Good; if you change your mind, let me know."

After Wren hung up, she said, "I'm going to check on the washer; it's probably close to finished, and I can throw the clothes into the dryer."

"While you're gone, my blanket and I will pull together breakfast for us; how's that?"

"That would be great; I'll be right back."

Rascal beat Wren to the door.

"You're a good boy, Rascal," Babette said.

When they neared the laundry room, Wren heard voices behind her; she and Rascal rushed into the laundry room. She removed the wet clothes from the washer and quickly tossed them in the dryer. After she started the dryer, the voices were louder.

*It's the same men.* Wren led Rascal into the restroom before she quietly closed and locked the door.

Wren listened. *They've stopped near the laundry room door.*

"So all we're supposed to do is scare the woman that's in the first cabin? Why? How are we going to do that?" The man coughed.

The man with the squeaky voice said, "I thought I told you to get cough drops. Did you know you ask too many questions for your own good? Lilith wants her out of here, and she said scaring her was the best way because someone else had already got the ball rolling. Do you know how to catch a raccoon or a snake, or something?"

"Me? No, I'm allergic. I do a pretty good owl hoot."

"That's creepy enough. Why don't you go into the woods and hoot. I'll throw some small rocks onto the roof; they'll sound like something scratching in an attic."

As they headed toward the cabin, the first man coughed repeatedly. After he caught his breath, he asked, "So, what are you thinking? Like ten minutes?"

"That's probably about right; then it will go all quiet, and that's creepy too."

"I heard there was an undercover cop nosing around. Is that why Lilith said no rough stuff?"

"Who knows?" the man squeaked.

Wren whispered, "Okay, Rascal, let's take a chance; you go first."

Rascal dashed to the fifth wheel while Wren ran as fast as she could. After they were inside, she was out of breath and leaned against the door.

"Are you okay?" Babette asked. "Sit down, and I'll give you a coffee refill. What happened?"

"While Rascal and I were in the laundry room..." Wren sipped her coffee while she told Babette about the two men and their orders from Lilith to scare Jake.

"Why would Lilith want to scare Jake?"

"They didn't know; one man said Lilith told him someone else tried to scare her, so it wouldn't take much for them to frighten her. They're obviously thugs, not critical thinkers."

Wren explained the men's plan to hoot like an owl and throw pebbles on the cabin roof while she set the table with forks and knives.

Babette shook her head as she set butter, strawberry jam, and syrup on the table then put French toast on their plates.

"Did you get the idea they've never been given an order to frighten someone without physical force involved?"

Wren smeared a little jam on her French toast then added a little syrup.

When Babette raised her eyebrows, Wren said, "I couldn't decide."

Babette shrugged and put jam and syrup on her French toast too.

Wren took her first bite. "Mmm, the French toast is delicious."

Babette nodded. "Love the jam and syrup."

After they finished their breakfast, Wren said, "I'm going to run to the laundry room before it gets any lighter; hopefully the thugs aren't still hanging around."

Wren exhaled before she opened the door; she raced to the laundry room with Rascal at her side. When she reached the building, Wren froze at the distinctive hoot of a barred owl: "who-cooks-for-you?"

She exhaled as she hurried into the laundry room. *That was an actual owl, not the thug.* Wren leaned against the dryer as it slowed then stopped while she caught her breath. While she emptied the machine, Wren said, "Let's go; this will definitely be enough exercise for me for the day, Rascal."

Wren grabbed her boots that were on the picnic bench before she and Rascal went inside. After Wren handed the dry clothes to Babette, she sat at the dining table to catch her breath again.

"Would more coffee help?" Babette asked.

Wren nodded while she continued to gasp for her breath.

Babette refilled Wren's cup. "I'll take the first shower; you relax."

Wren exhaled then sipped her coffee. "Good."

When Babette came out of the shower, she said, "Your turn; will you have to wait for the hot water to recover?"

"The water heater is on demand, so the water is heated as needed; there isn't any hot water stored on board. The fifth wheel is my dream camper; it has all the things I love." Wren smiled.

After Wren's shower, she dressed in clean clothes and hung her towel over the shower stall before she hugged the pillow again then made the bed. Before she joined Babette, Wren texted Justin. "See you soon."

Justin replied, "Can't wait, sweetheart!"

When she joined Babette in the living area, Babette smiled as she folded up the sofa bed. "We do clean up right nice, don't we? It's light outside, but it's still pretty early. Are you ready to drop me off at my house?"

"I can do that, but what's the pickup plan?"

Babette furrowed her brow. "I don't think it would be wise for you to hang close, so why don't you head back to the campground; I'll text you where to pick me up."

"Okay, but I need to know when to panic if I haven't heard from you." Wren frowned.

"I'll text you within thirty minutes after you drop me off with a status; how's that?"

Wren nodded. "If I don't hear from you within thirty minutes, I'm calling in the posse."

Babette rolled her eyes. "You play dirty, Wren."

Wren giggled. "That's the nicest thing anyone has ever said to me."

Babette slipped on her swamp boots. "I'd like to travel with only what I'll need, so I'll stick my house and car keys in my pocket, but leave this heavy ring of office keys here."

"We're ready when you are." Wren grabbed her backpack and her phone.

Babette turned off the light over the stove, and Wren opened the door. Rascal dashed out and waited next to the truck.

"When I open the door for Rascal, be ready to jump in behind him; after I close the truck door, I'll lock the trailer."

After she locked the trailer door, Wren turned on the road that went to Babette's house.

"Are you sure this is a good idea? I'm having second thoughts." Wren said.

"Now that you've said something, so am I," Babette said.

"Is there somewhere I can wait without being too noticeable that is close enough for you to walk? Better yet, is there somewhere I could park my truck and go with you? You need someone to watch your back."

Babette furrowed her brow. "Not really; since it's daylight, I could walk faster from my house to the campground by going through the swamp than I could to where you were parked; if you were with me, you'd slow me down in the swamp, and you know it. Let's stick with our original plan."

Babette's phone buzzed a text. "Oh, no."

Wren slowed her truck. "Is something wrong? Do I need to pull over?"

Babette exhaled. "Sorry; I got a text from a friend who said Al was attacked late last night." Babette's voice had a catch in it. "Al was attacked in front of his house last night. He's in the hospital, but the worst thing was the attackers stomped on his right hand."

"Al, the fiddler?"

"That's right; the thugs were waiting for him; he told them he wasn't paying them another dime."

When Babette said, "Slow down; drop me off at the mailbox ahead."

"Are you sure about this?" Wren said.

"No, but there's no one else."

After Wren dropped off Babette near her house, she headed back to the campground. "I really am uneasy about leaving Babette."

When Wren reached the campground twenty minutes later, she said, "We should be hearing from Babette any time now."

Wren's eyes widened. "Rascal, Mara is at the trailer."

After Wren parked and opened the door for Rascal, Mara motioned for Wren to follow her, held up her hand, and pointed at Wren's shoes.

"Do you want me to change my shoes to boots?" Wren asked.

Mara stood motionless.

"She does, doesn't she, Rascal?"

Wren went inside the trailer; after she put on her boots and a jacket, she grabbed her backpack and locked the door behind her.

Mara motioned for Wren to follow her; when a sudden gust whistled through the treetops, Wren was certain the wind told her to hurry.

Mara raced toward the swamp then turned and waited until Wren was close before she darted ahead into the cypress.

Wren lost sight of her. "Where did she go, Rascal?"

Rascal disappeared then barked. When Wren reached Rascal, Mara was waiting with him.

Mara disappeared, and Rascal followed her then barked. As Wren hurried to find Rascal she grumbled, "I have no clue where or which way I'm going."

When Wren caught up with them, she asked, "Can't you lead me where you want me to go instead of making me run after you?"

Mara's mouth twitched; when she disappeared, Rascal raced after her.

Wren exhaled. "The answer must be no."

Rascal barked then continued to bark with a sense of urgency.

Wren stumbled over a cypress root in her rush to get to Rascal. When she tried to grab onto a tree to avoid the knees, she felt something move under her fingers. Wren screamed and let go of the tree and splashed as she fell into the shallow, mucky water.

Wren grabbed onto the nearest knee and pulled herself up. She shuddered as she tried to brush away the dripping slime on her arms.

Rascal rushed to her and whined.

"I'm okay; where am I supposed to go?"

Rascal led Wren a little farther before he yipped.

Mara pointed to the right, and Wren stepped through the trees then hurried to Babette who was slumped on her left side against a cypress stump as she sat in the wet marsh. She had an abrasion and a large lump on the right side of her forehead, and the right side of her face from her eye to her mouth was swollen.

Wren knelt next to her and the rotten egg smell of the decomposing organic matter in the muck took away her breath. "Babette, can you hear me?"

Babette moaned.

"It's okay, don't talk."

Wren pulled out her phone, but she didn't have any bars.

"Dang phone," Wren grumbled as she waded through the shallow water until she was behind Babette.

"I want to get you out of the water; let me know if I hurt you." She slipped her arms under Babette's arms then wrapped her arms around Babette's chest to brace Babette against her body; when Wren leaned back to drag her to dry land, Babette cried out in pain.

Wren quickly stopped pulling and loosened her grip. "I'm so sorry; is it your ribs?"

Tears rolled down Babette's left cheek as she nodded. Babette moaned and pointed to the dry grass.

Wren's eyes welled up. "Are you saying you still want me to pull you out of the water?"

Babette nodded.

"Are you sure, Babette?"

Babette mumbled a single sound then emphatically nodded.

"I'll be as careful as I can." Wren slipped her arms under Babette's arms as she curled hers up and back. When she pulled Babette away from the tree, Babette whimpered, and tears rolled down Wren's cheeks. After Wren had dragged Babette to dry ground, she stopped near a large tree.

Babette groaned as she exhaled and leaned against the tree. Wren sat next to her and gasped for breath from the exertion and stress.

Rascal whined; when Wren glanced up, Mara disappeared, and Rascal followed her.

"Rascal must have gone for help." Wren slowed her breathing. "Are we close to your house?"

Babette nodded and mumbled as she struggled to rise.

"I didn't exactly understand you; are you trying to get to your feet?"

Babette nodded.

"Are you sure? I don't know how I can help you," Wren said.

Wren stooped to lift Babette under her arms, but she didn't have the right leverage to help Babette to her feet. Wren exhaled. "That didn't work; we need to try something else."

Babette groaned and forced out one simple word. "Call."

"You want me to call Armand?"

Babette nodded.

"I didn't have any bars at all earlier." Wren slowly checked her phone and sighed in relief. "I have a signal; it's only one bar, but I can try a text."

Wren sent a text to Armand. "Guppy. B hurt in the swamp near her house. R went for help."

Wren held her breath then exhaled when Armand replied.

Wren read the text aloud. "Got it; on my way."

When Babette tried to speak, she wheezed but immediately clutched her ribs as she coughed. After she regained her breath, she pointed at her feet.

"You don't want to try to stand up again, do you?" Wren asked.

Babette vigorously shook her head and moaned as she pointed to her feet and mumbled, "Uff."

"Off? You want your boots off?"

Babette slowly nodded once.

Wren watched Babette's face for any additional signs of pain as she carefully removed Babette's left boot.

"Uff."

"Do you want your sock off too?" Wren asked.

Babette quietly breathed out the word. "Yeah."

When Wren removed Babette's sock she gazed at Babette. "There are folded papers wrapped in plastic inside your sock, but the paper got soggy. Were you hiding it?"

Babette nodded and pointed to her bare foot.

"You want me to put on your sock and boot? They're wet."

Babette shook her finger for emphasis as she pointed; Wren shrugged then put Babette's soggy sock and boot back on Babette's foot.

Babette pointed to her other foot. "Uff."

After Wren removed the boot and sock, she found another set of papers folded and wrapped in plastic. Wren returned the sock and boot to Babette's foot.

Babette muttered, "Hi."

Wren furrowed her brow. *Hi?* "Did you want me to hide the papers like you did? Are you sure?"

Babette groaned and nodded.

Wren removed her wet boots and socks and stuck a packet inside each of her socks and growled as she struggled with putting back on her soggy, cold socks. After Wren put on her boots, Babette sighed.

Wren's phone buzzed a text. "Armand says he's close. Do I tell him about the papers?"

Babette whimpered as she shook her head.

"Should I look at them first? Are these the papers Simone hid for you?"

Babette nodded.

Rascal barked nearby.

"Here, boy," Wren called out.

Mara stood next to a nearby tree while Rascal dashed to Wren and smothered her with kisses; she hugged him. "Good boy, Rascal."

Wren smiled at Mara. "Thanks."

Mara stared at the ground then disappeared.

Armand rushed to Babette.

"Her ribs may be broken, Armand," Wren said. "She tried to talk to me, but her mouth is so swollen…"

Armand carefully lifted his sister with ease. "I have my truck at her house; I'll drop you off at the campground before I take Babette to the hospital."

Babette sighed as she leaned against her brother's chest.

Wren had to scramble to keep up with Armand's wide stride; Rascal trailed alongside her.

When they reached Armand's old truck, Wren opened the passenger's door, and Armand eased Babette into the seat.

After he closed the door, Armand strode to the rear of the truck and lowered the tailgate. "The only place I have for you and Rascal to ride is the bed of the truck, Wren."

Rascal leaped into the back of the truck, and Armand helped Wren climb in before he raised the tailgate.

"Sit close to the cab and face backwards; less wind will hit your face."

As Armand headed down the driveway toward the road, Wren wrapped her arms around Rascal. "I've never ridden in the back of a pickup. I feel very daring."

When Armand was on the road, he sped up. Wren smiled at the thrill that went down her spine.

Armand lowered his window when he stopped on the road across from the campground driveway. "Can you and Rascal hop out here?"

Wren used the trailer hitch on the back of the truck as a step and climbed out; after she lowered the tailgate, Rascal jumped out too. She raised the tailgate before they crossed the road.

When Wren waved, Armand made a U-turn and headed into town.

"That was exciting, Rascal; I'm not sure Justin would agree, except he wouldn't be surprised because he's probably getting used to us doing unusual things."

While Wren and Rascal strolled down the driveway, Wren's phone buzzed a text from Justin.

"Morning meeting is over. Ok to call?"

Wren called him. "How was your meeting?"

"I expected it to be mostly rehashing of the conference, but I was impressed with the quality of the comments. I have a list of suggestions for improvement that Pat and I can discuss and maybe prioritize for Hidden Gulch. What's your morning been like?"

# Chapter Ten

Wren furrowed her brow. *Where do I start?*

"We've been pretty busy; Rascal and I are taking a much-needed walk in the sunshine." Wren told him about overhearing the men when they talked about Jake.

Justin chuckled. "Did they scare her off?"

"I don't know; Rascal and I dropped off Babette at her house then..."

Justin interrupted. "My favorite elevator's here; I'll talk to you later. Love you, sweetheart." He hung up.

Wren exhaled. "The elevator at the hotel saved me from telling Justin our long, convoluted story about getting lost in the swamp and finding Babette."

She stopped to watch a great blue heron as it flew overhead; before she continued her walk, Wren listened to an unseen bird that sounded like it was high in the top of one of the nearby trees. Wren tried to mimic its call. "Kee-aah, kee-aah, kee-aah."

Rascal stared at her then snorted.

"I'm pretty sure it's a red-shouldered hawk; maybe I could whistle its call."

While Wren tried to copy the hawk by whistling, Rascal raced ahead to the campground.

"It wasn't that bad, you critic," Wren grumbled as she trudged alone to the trailer.

When she reached the end of the driveway, Naomi and Jake were in front of the registration office. Naomi's arms were crossed as Jake waved her arms.

*Jake is obviously complaining about something.* Wren turned at the first row of campsites and strolled away from the office. When she reached the end of the row, she heard the roar of a car engine as it sped toward the exit; Wren turned quickly enough to see Jake leaving the campground.

When she reached the trailer, she smiled at Rascal who was relaxing in the shade under the trailer as he waited for her. "Are you coming in with me?"

Rascal followed Wren inside and took a long drink; while she leaned against the wall, she took off her boots and pulled off her socks. She put her stinky socks in a plastic bag and put the packets on the counter. After she quickly stripped and put her soaked, smelly clothes in the plastic bag with the socks, Wren showered.

After she was dressed, Wren brushed her hair then carried the plastic bag and her boots outside. She dropped her sack in the truck bed before she rinsed off her boots and set them on the picnic bench to dry.

When she went inside the camper, she poured a glass of sweet tea, picked up the packets, and sat at the dining table.

After Wren gulped down half of her glass of tea, she carefully peeled away the plastic from one of the soggy papers and gently pried open the first fold. She inspected the sodden mess and set it on the table.

"I'll have to let this dry before I tackle the rest of it, or it will be completely unreadable."

After she drank the rest of her tea, she delicately removed the plastic from the second set then set it on the table. Wren inspected the wet papers. "You need better circulation."

She pulled out the rack from the oven and set it on top of the stove. Wren turned on the fan that was in the hood over the stove before she put the two wet parcels on the rack.

She crossed her arms and gazed at the papers.

After a few minutes, Wren headed for the door. "Watching paper dry is as exciting as watching grass grow. Let's see if Naomi feels like telling us what sent Jake off the deep end, not that it's any of our business."

Rascal growled.

"I forgot you're not a fan of Naomi and her cats. You can wait on the porch and greet any dog people."

Rascal rose from the rug where he had been relaxing and stretched. Wren opened the door. "I'll put out the awning, and we can sit in the shade for a while before lunch. Have you noticed how slowly this day is dragging?"

When they reached the office, Rascal flopped onto the porch at the end farthest from the door. Wren rolled her eyes as she reached for the doorknob. When the knob wouldn't turn, she tried again.

"That's funny," Wren said. "The door is locked, but Naomi's car is here, and the lights are on. Do you suppose she accidentally locked it?"

Wren shaded her eyes as she peered inside; when she didn't see any movement, she tapped lightly on the glass with her knuckles.

She shrugged. "Naomi must be cleaning the restrooms or picking up trash; it makes sense for her to lock the door while she's gone. We can head back to the trailer, go for a walk, or check the dog park; it's your choice, Rascal."

Before Wren stepped off the porch, Rascal growled, and the office door flew open.

"Sorry, Wren. I didn't realize I'd left the door locked when I came in this morning; although I'm glad you're my first visitor, not anyone else. I'd be horrified if any of our new guests found the door locked. Come on in; did you need something in particular?"

Wren followed Naomi into the office. "I don't remember seeing any, but my best friend's birthday is next week, and I thought authentic Mardi Gras beads would be a surprise for her."

"We used to carry them, but we don't anymore." Naomi smiled. "One of our out-of-state guests told Babette everybody knows the only authentic beads come from the French Quarter in New Orleans."

"Oh, no." Wren raised her eyebrows. "What did Babette say?"

Naomi chuckled. "Babette thanked her for the hot tip."

Wren giggled. "That was the perfect response, wasn't it?"

"That wasn't all; Babette sold the woman six Cranky Crawfish T-shirts to take home to her family and friends as souvenirs."

"Now, that's an idea; do you have any Cranky Crawfish oven mitts or dish towels?"

"We don't, but maybe we should; I'll mention it to Babette."

"I'll look around for a minute or two; don't let me keep you from working," Wren said as she wandered to a rack of postcards.

"If you don't mind, I did get a little behind this morning." Naomi turned toward the registration computer. "Did I tell you about the woman in the first cabin? In the first place, she flashed a badge when she registered and asked for a discount. When I tried to engage her in a polite conversation, she bit my head off and implied she was undercover. If she was undercover, then why did she ask for a discount? She definitely got under my skin."

"I can see why; she sounds really obnoxious," Wren said.

"It gets worse." Naomi growled, "A few minutes ago, she screamed at me and claimed there was a dead rat in the cabin, and she wanted a full refund and additional compensation to pay for another place for her to stay."

"What? That's too bizarre. A mouse, maybe, but a rat? She sounds delusional."

Naomi glowered. "It took everything I had to keep from asking her who she thought she was. When I told her if she'd show me where it was, I would take care of it right away; she practically bit my head off because she told me there was no way she would return to that vermin-infested building. I hurried to her cabin with her right on my heels while she told me how incompetent I was. You probably won't be surprised that there was nothing there. When I came out, she accused me of hiding it and cussed me the entire way back to the office." Naomi clenched her fists.

"That's terrible."

"She told me her fiancé would be here later today, and he would settle her bill. If she only knew..." Naomi's voice trailed off.

"Knew what?" Wren asked.

Naomi cleared her throat. "How awful she sounded."

Wren nodded. *That's not what you were going to say.* "I'm really sorry she was so horribly rude to you."

"Thank you, Wren."

As Wren turned to leave, she glanced back at Naomi before she left the office; Wren's brow furrowed. *Why was Naomi smiling? Is she going to charge Jake extra for the day?*

On their way back to the trailer, Rascal stopped and yipped at the cabins. Wren gaped at Mara who stood in front of the first cabin; she was swinging a dead rat by its tail. After she expertly flung the carcass into the woods, Wren glanced up at the circling black vultures overhead and the lone turkey vulture in a tree who swooped to where the rat landed.

Mara waved then disappeared.

Wren laughed. "It's time for lunch. I'll fix a sandwich and dine with the vultures."

Wren brought her sandwich and lidded tumbler of sweet tea outside and sat in the awning's shade with Rascal by her side. When new campers rolled past the trailer, Wren waved and nodded as a light breeze kept away the bugs.

"This is how camping's supposed to be, isn't it, Rascal?"

After she finished eating, Wren rose and dusted off the crumbs from her shirt and lap.

"I need a cookie. How do you feel about a ride to the Cranky Crawfish? I assume the engagement party will be called off; we could pick up something for supper that I could warm up."

Wren retracted the awning before they left. On the way to the Cranky Crawfish, she said, "I read it's important to never leave an awning extended when you're away from the campground, because you never know when the wind will decide to change from a breeze to a gale."

After Wren parked in the shade, Rascal trotted to flop down on the porch next to his friend, the wooden bear.

While Wren gazed at the cookies and brownies in the bakery display case, she froze at the sound of a dry, hacking cough when two men came into the Cranky Crawfish.

"Cover your mouth when you cough," the man with the squeaky, grating voice said. "We'll grab something to eat on the road."

"I don't get why we can't sit at a table and eat like normal people," the other man said. "I been wanting me some good jambalaya, not a sandwich we could get at any gas station."

"She said we had to leave immediately because you botched the job on the girl."

"Yeah, but I heard her rip you a new one over that smashing stunt."

Wren raised her eyebrows. *Smashing stunt?*

"I was on the phone with her; you wasn't." The man's squeaky voice rose an octave. "You don't know what she said.

We'll get something then stop up the road somewhere and eat; is that good enough for you?"

The man nodded as he coughed.

"Tell me what you want, and I'll order for us while you wait outside."

"I'll wait in the car; that stray dog on the porch snarled at me when we got out of the car. Give me the keys."

"Let's sit down and eat; we'll draw less attention than if we're hanging around waiting for our order. Get yourself some cough drops; we can't sit in the restaurant with you barking like a seal."

Wren snorted. *I knew he wouldn't give you the keys.*

The bakery clerk smiled. "Have you decided what you want? No rush, but I didn't want you to feel neglected."

"I need a dozen cookies, but I don't know what kind."

"Our two best sellers are our new toasted coconut pecan cookie and a long-time favorite, our dark chocolate chip cookie with pecans. How about a half dozen of both?"

"That's a logical, tasty solution."

"What else can I get you?" The clerk slid open the display case.

"I thought I heard someone mention takeout; do you have a menu?"

The clerk rolled her eyes. "The only takeout you'll get here is if you don't clean your plate, our chef may allow you to take your meager leftovers home, but only if you insist."

Wren smiled. "I heard of a chef who didn't allow leftovers to leave his restaurant. He told his guests to come back when they were hungry, and he'd cook them a fresh meal."

While the clerk loaded a small, white bakery box with cookies, she returned Wren's smile. "They're probably cousins; however, I can tell you the special tonight is crawfish etouffee."

"That's wonderful; it's my favorite; I'm not sure my...friend has tried it, but I'm certain he'll love it."

After the clerk set the box of cookies on the counter, she gazed at Wren. "Honey, we all know about the marshal; friends are good, but isn't he more than a friend?"

Wren handed the clerk her credit card and exhaled. "You're right; I don't want to rush anything and scare him off."

The clerk raised her eyebrows as she completed the transaction. "Well, when you and this random friend of yours come for dinner this evening, tell him to park in the back; it's where the locals park. Oh, and come in the back door for priority seating family style with the locals."

Wren furrowed her brow. "It's time for me to have a chat with the marshal, isn't it?"

The clerk returned Wren's credit card and handed her the receipt and the cookies. "Clearing the air is always a good move, don't you think? I know y'all will enjoy the cookies."

Wren heard a hacking cough when she passed by the restaurant host stand; she paused briefly to peer at the tables, but she didn't see the men.

Rascal joined her after she was outside; Wren scanned the parking lot on the way to her truck then narrowed her eyes at the car that had nosed into a spot across from her truck.

After she opened the back door for Rascal to jump in, she snapped a photo of the car's license plate. She started the engine before she texted Justin. "Call?"

Her phone rang immediately.

"Are you okay, honey?" Justin asked.

"Rascal and I are at the Cranky Crawfish. Two men attacked Babette this morning, and the fiddler was attacked last night, and his hand was smashed. I think the two men are in the restaurant for lunch. I took a snapshot of their license plate."

Justin's tone of voice turned hard. "Text me the photo; I'll call you right back after I talk to Vic, so you can fill me in with everything you know." Justin hung up.

Wren sent the text, and a minute later, her phone rang.

"What can you tell me?" Justin asked.

"When two men came into the Cranky Crawfish, I recognized their voices because they were at the campground late last night, and I heard them talking outside the trailer. Last night, they mentioned Lilith; it sounded like they were supposed to find Babette. Just now, they were arguing when they came into the store; one man said that a woman, and I'm sure he was talking about Lilith, told him they had to leave immediately because the other man had botched the job on the girl. After the second man mentioned the other guy was in trouble for the smashing stunt, I realized they were talking about Babette and Al, the fiddler."

"Where are you?"

"Still in the parking lot. I texted you as soon as Rascal and I were in the truck."

Justin growled, "Did they see you? Leave now; text me when you're at the campground."

"They didn't see me; I was at the bakery counter."

"Good." He hung up.

Wren backed out of her parking space and headed toward the campground. "I forgot to tell Justin, but I just remembered the men saw you because one man said you snarled at him."

Wren glanced back at Rascal, who grinned.

After they returned and went inside the trailer, Wren sent a text to Justin. "At the campground."

He replied, "Thanks. Be safe."

Wren opened the bakery box and pulled out a chocolate chip cookie.

While she munched on her dessert, she said, "All I wanted was a cookie after lunch; we didn't expect to run into any bad guys, did we?"

Rascal circled his rug then flopped down and closed his eyes.

Wren turned over the damp papers before she carefully unfolded them a third time. *They'll be dry enough to read later.*

Wren turned on her laptop to check her email. "Rascal, Kendra sent me her edits."

Rascal twitched in his sleep while Wren added Kendra's edits to her final document then added a note at the end dedicating the article to Simone.

Wren composed an email to Charlie, attached the document, and clicked send. "There you go, Charlie; the last article about haunted campgrounds."

Wren opened the draft of her novel then stared blankly at the page for a few minutes. "Aha, I remember where I was going with that."

Her fingers flew across the keyboard as she wrote. After two hours, her phone rang.

"Hi, honey, we left the parking garage and are now sitting in traffic; where are you?" Justin asked.

Wren rolled her eyes. "You said that like I'm always somewhere I shouldn't be. We're in the trailer for your information; Rascal's asleep, and I'm working on my novel like any other normal author."

"Normal?" Justin snorted. "Any response I could make would get me into trouble. I called to give you an unofficial update. The deputy missed the two guys at the Cranky Crawfish. They ordered their meals, but one man had a terrible cough, so the manager offered to box up their order when it was ready; the men thanked her and left with their food not long after you called me. Their car description and the license number from your photo will be a tremendous help in finding them; they won't get far."

"I'm sorry they weren't still there," Wren said.

"I'm not; it's better their arrest is away from the Mahoneville area. Their license plate doesn't match the car, so they've made it easier on us."

Wren began pacing. "When will you be here?"

"Vic said it depends on the time of day and the day of the week; normally it's a two-hour drive, but the Friday traffic will make it closer to three or more."

Wren smiled. "I can't wait."

"Neither can I, sweetie."

After they hung up, Rascal nosed the front door. Wren put on her Cranky Crawfish ball cap and sunglasses, and they went outside.

"Where do you want to go, Rascal?"

Rascal whined then headed toward the dog park; Wren followed him. When they were close, Rascal trotted to the fence and went nose-to-nose with an English Springer Spaniel.

A lean man with unruly gray hair and a gray bushy mustache leaned on his cane as he called out, "Can I let your lab into the dog park? Gilly's not quite a year old, but she loves to play."

"Rascal would love it." Wren smiled as Rascal casually walked to the gate.

When the man opened the gate, Rascal sauntered inside. Gilly rushed to greet him and lunged downward into the bow that was the doggie let's-play position; Rascal lunged back, and Gilly zoomed around the dog park fence while Rascal sat and watched.

The man laughed as sat on the bench. "Rascal is smart. I wear out watching her zoomies."

After four rounds, Gilly returned to Rascal and lunged; when he returned the lunge, Gilly raced away and around the fence five more times. At the end of her set, the man called her to the water bowl near the faucet. After she drank her fill, Gilly trotted to Rascal and flopped down in the grass next to him.

The old man groaned as he rose with the assistance of his cane.

"Come, Gilly." He clicked the clip on the leash; Gilly tilted her head and gazed at Rascal. The man clicked the clip again, and Gilly wiggled her way to him.

"Good girl," he cooed as he snapped the leash to her collar. Before he opened the gate, he turned to Rascal and gave a nod. "We enjoyed your company, Rascal." He smiled at Wren. "You too, Miss."

After the man and Gilly reached their RV and went inside, Wren sat on the bench while Rascal investigated the dog park. Rascal trotted to the far end of the park and whined.

Desirada smiled. "No sneaking up on you, Rascal."

Rascal rushed to Wren to wait until Desirada came inside the dog park.

"She's getting bolder, sha." Desirada sat next to Wren. "When are you leaving again?"

"Probably Sunday."

Desirada nodded. "That's good."

Desirada whispered when she continued, "Al was careful; only a few of us knew."

Wren tilted her head and matched Desirada's quiet tone. "Knew what?"

"There are a few brave souls who are digging into the real purpose behind her protection scheme because we're convinced she has to be after more than the few pennies folks around here can scrape up."

Desirada rose. "The stakes must be high because she is becoming more dangerous; I'm afraid she'll decide you're a threat, so it's good that y'all are leaving soon."

Desirada stopped at the gate. "Our girl's got your back, Wren; you've been wise to trust her."

"Do you mean Mara?" Wren asked.

Desirada limped away without answering.

"I was hoping Desirada would tell me more about Mara." Wren exhaled. "Ready to go back to the trailer, Rascal?"

When they reached the trailer, her phone rang. "Pat's calling, Rascal."

She answered as they went inside.

"I talked to Justin, Wren; he asked me to call you and fill you in because he's on the road with the sheriff," Pat said. "I know people change, but Cody and I couldn't put together how the Jake who had visited her grandmother as a young girl and was so well-liked in Hidden Gulch could be the same Jake who is stalking the marshal. I haven't seen her grandmother in quite a while because she moved to assisted living six or seven years ago when it was discovered she was in the stages of early dementia. When I visited her right after Jake quit and asked about Jake, she became very agitated and wailed that her last relative, her sweet granddaughter Jake, was dead. The assisted living records show Jake's last visit was five years ago."

Wren began pacing. "This doesn't make any sense."

Pat sighed. "Cody and I couldn't let it go. An aide at the assisted living told me Jake was living in Colorado Springs the last time she visited her grandmother, so I contacted an old friend in the Colorado State Police who told me Jake had died in a hiking accident almost five years ago. After I told him about the current Jake, he said he'd check into the details and get back to me."

"What?" Wren's knees grew weak; she plumped down on the sofa. "What about fingerprints and ID?"

"I have very little other than the earliest record of fingerprints that I could find for Jake was two years ago when she was accepted into the police academy. I've turned over my findings to the FBI."

"So the new Jake is the one who harassed a student in the police academy and may have killed a man, right?" Wren asked.

"That's what Cody and I think. I have a call scheduled later today with that other student who continued his career in law enforcement in Texas; he may have additional information that will help us, but I can at least let him know he made the right choice to leave Arizona. I didn't say anything to Justin, but Cody went to Colorado Springs on Wednesday to do some informal checking on his own."

"I have so many questions about the two Jakes," Wren said.

"So do we, which is why Cody went to Colorado." Pat cleared his throat. "Cody is convinced that Jake is a psychopathic killer, which is why she is particularly attracted to anyone who is nice to her, and I don't disagree. Cody sent me a text earlier with some information; he doesn't have anything except hearsay, but he will probably call you later today, so I won't be in the middle."

"Cody's good at digging into the details, isn't he?" Wren smiled.

Pat chuckled. "That shyster lawyer is turning into my favorite person; don't tell Justin I said that."

After they hung up, Wren began pacing. "Do you think the voodoo doll and the dead rat were enough to scare away Jake, Rascal?"

She sat in front of her computer and searched for "psychopathic killer." After Wren carefully reviewed several sources, she exhaled. "I see why Cody said she was a psychopath because she definitely fits the profile; if she saw the voodoo doll and the dead rat as things outside of her control that might explain her extremely angry reaction, but I don't know if it was enough to keep her away, and I'm totally outside my realm of expertise, anyway."

After Wren closed her laptop, she leaned back and moaned. "That didn't help at all; I'm going to the office to see if Naomi has any Jake updates. Do you want to go?"

Rascal growled as he lumbered to the door.

"You don't have to go if you want to stay here."

Rascal kept his nose pointed at the door.

"Well, let's go."

Rascal flopped down on the porch in his usual spot away from the door; as Wren approached the door, she heard Naomi growl, "Off the road is fine; do what you have to do."

When Wren opened the door, Naomi slammed her phone on the counter as she muttered, "Incompetent fools."

Naomi smiled as Wren went inside. "Lost my temper for a second; I'm having some work done on my driveway, and it's not going as smoothly as I hoped, but you're not here to listen to my complaints. What can I do for you, Wren?"

"I'm low on the chemical for the black water holding tank; do you have any?"

"Right over there on the wall." Naomi pointed. "Do you know what kind you want?"

"Sure do." Wren examined the chemicals and picked out the brand and type her dad usually bought.

When Wren put the package on the counter, Naomi said, "I am definitely having a rough day; how's your day going?"

Wren smiled. "Rascal and I spent most of the morning at the dog park; it really is one of the best we've seen."

"That's nice to hear." Naomi frowned at her phone when it rang then picked it up and silenced it.

# Chapter Eleven

Wren glanced toward the consignment shelf then peered more closely. "Are there some new items on the craft shelf?"

"There certainly are; I should have told you. One of our craft ladies dropped off a few items; see if there's anything you'd like."

"Thanks, I'd love to." Wren strolled to the shelf and admired the new earrings and bracelets. "She's really talented, isn't she?"

Naomi's phone rang again, and Wren picked up a necklace to examine more closely.

Naomi glanced at Wren before she answered her phone and stepped outside to talk. When Rascal growled, she hurried back inside and returned to the registration desk.

She tapped her pen on the pad next to the computer then doodled while she listened.

"Well done; is there any damage to the truck?"

Wren picked up the pair of earrings that matched the necklace.

Naomi continued doodling. "It's a relief to have one less worry, or in this case two. Yep, the usual."

After she hung up, Naomi said, "Crisis averted."

Wren glanced up. "I'm sorry; did you say something?"

"Just talking to myself; bad habit." Naomi exhaled. "More driveway problems solved; maybe it's a good day after all."

"I like the necklace; I'm going to think about it, if that's okay." Wren returned the necklace and earrings to the shelf.

Naomi rung up the chemical. "That's fine. All her work is custom; she's a gifted artisan, isn't she?"

Wren nodded as she paid for her purchase.

"I heard from Miss Fancy Pants." Naomi put the chemical into a bag and handed Wren the receipt. "She said she regretted being so short with me; I must admit I was surprised by the call and by an apology. Anyway, she claimed she'll be back later to clear out her things and pay through tomorrow. I got the impression that she didn't plan to stay here this evening, but I didn't ask. I'm not convinced she'll actually show up, but I'll still wait until tomorrow to clean the cabin."

Before Wren picked up the sack with the chemical, the man from the dog park came into the store. He smiled. "We knew you were in here because we saw Rascal. Gilly's relaxing with her buddy on the porch; I'm not sure I've ever seen her so calm. Rascal has made quite an impression on her."

He turned to Naomi. "Your dog park is wonderful; we're running low on dog food. What brands do you carry?"

"We carry the best." Naomi smiled as she led him to the shelf with the dog food. "We also have a refrigerated brand, if that's what your Gilly prefers."

As Wren picked up the sack with the chemical, she glanced at Naomi's doodling and rolled her eyes. *She's hung two stick figures on a gallows. I'll bet one is Jake; I wonder who the second one is.*

Before Wren reached the door, the man asked, "Do you mind waiting a second? Gilly would enjoy walking back with Rascal, if you don't mind a little company."

Wren smiled. "That would be great."

After he paid for his purchase, he picked up the dog food, and they left the office.

Gilly watched Rascal; when he rose, she jumped up.

As Wren strolled alongside the slower pace of the older man, Rascal and Gilly raced to the dog park then back. Rascal led Gilly on a chase around the campground before he stopped at the dog park.

The man said, "Gilly will sleep well tonight."

"So will Rascal."

"I know about the fishing hole," the old man said.

Wren stopped and stared at him.

He chuckled. "I retired five years ago, but kind of semi-unretired at Armand's request. He thought it would work better for you if you knew you had a nearby backup at the campground."

"Wow," Wren said. "I appreciate it."

"Armand said you'd like to know Babette's going to be in the hospital a couple more days, but she's fine, and it's okay to mention me to Justin."

They continued walking.

"What can I do to help?" Wren asked.

The man smiled. "Since I'm your onsite backup, I'd appreciate it if you didn't get hurt or killed; it would look bad on my heretofore impressive resume."

Wren giggled. "I'll add that to my list. What do I call you?"

"Armand calls me Shamus; it was my preretirement name at work."

"Thank you, Shamus."

When they reached the dog park, the man opened the gate; Rascal trotted inside, and Gilly followed him. Rascal yipped, and Gilly zoomed around the fence.

As Wren and Shamus sat on the bench, Wren's phone rang.

Shamus motioned toward the gate. "Go ahead; Rascal will help me watch Gilly."

As Wren walked away from the dog park toward the trailer, she answered, "Hello, Cody."

"I have this urge to tell you not to shoot me," Cody said.

Wren snorted. "Duly noted."

"Good; I met with some of the real Jake's friends. Jake had a new friend, Deb, that none of her close friends liked very much. Jake and her friends enjoyed hiking, and Deb joined them. The friends said that Deb monopolized more and more of Jake's time to the point of excluding the friends. One friend had two photos she took of Jake and Deb without Deb's knowledge. One is the first time the friends met Deb, and the second one is two months later. I'll send them to you, but in the second photo, Deb is deeply tanned and has long, dark dyed hair. The resemblance to Jake is uncanny."

"How did Jake die?"

"The friend said they all went hiking; she said they always stayed together when they hiked, but Deb talked Jake into taking a shortcut to beat everyone to the top. The friend offered to go along because Deb was not a strong climber, but Deb claimed the friend was jealous, so Jake laughed and told the friend the two of them would be waiting at the top."

"I'm not a climber, but that doesn't sound safe for someone to embark on a tough, off-path climb with an inexperienced person."

"You're right; when the friends got to the top, Jake and Deb were not there. They waited and searched for an hour before they found Deb, who was in a state of collapse; however, the friend said Deb's emotional state was too perfectly performed to be believable. Deb told them Jake had slipped and fallen into a crevice. While one friend called for a rescue team, two of the stronger climbers descended at the point where Deb claimed Jake had fallen, but they couldn't find her. A recovery party found her three days later, about a half mile away from where Deb said she'd fallen. According to the coroner, Jake died from exposure, not from the fall. Deb made it all about her with a huge fuss about how devastated she was that her friend died because the other hikers refused to accompany her. It goes without saying the friends were livid."

"I would think so; that's horrible."

"The friends knew Jake didn't have any living family except for her grandmother, so after Deb left Colorado a week later, they paid for Jake's funeral and cremation and scattered Jake's ashes on the mountain she loved. As far as ID is concerned, the friend was certain Deb took Jake's ID and emptied her bank accounts over the two months before Jake died because Jake's saving and checking accounts had balances of less than two hundred dollars."

"She could have also obtained an Arizona ID during that time too," Wren added.

"Yes, and established Arizona residency. I've turned over what I have to the FBI; they'll get copies of the coroner's report and death certificate for starters." Cody cleared his throat. "Do you know where the phony Jake is now?"

"She had an argument with the campground manager and left, but the campground manager told me Jake might return to pay her bill, but she didn't know when and sounded doubtful."

"When will Justin arrive? Soon?"

Wren checked the time. "In less than an hour, depending on traffic. Do you think she came here to kill him?"

"I don't know; from what I can tell, her specialty is to make her murders look like accidents. Is Justin driving your truck?"

"No, he's riding with the local sheriff in the sheriff's cruiser."

"She's never committed a murder with witnesses, at least she didn't with the four that I know about."

"Four?"

"Jake plus the three deaths Pat and I discovered since she came to Arizona; I don't know about any others in Colorado, but the FBI is looking."

Wren swallowed hard. "What can I do?"

Cody chuckled. "Do your Wren thing; that's what you'd do anyway no matter what I said."

After they hung up, Wren strolled back to the dog park while she thought about Cody's findings.

After she sat on the bench with Shamus, he examined her face. "Is everything okay?"

"It's complicated." Wren exhaled.

Shamus nodded. "I'm a whiz at one-thousand-piece puzzles."

Wren stared at him. "Give me a second."

Wren rose from the bench and paced then sent Armand a text. "Manatee in sight. Is Gilly's friend my backup? Okay to trust?"

Armand replied immediately. "Absolutely."

Wren returned to the bench. "Justin's senior deputy and I think a psychopathic killer is stalking Justin."

"Tell me about him."

"He's a she." Wren quickly summarized what she knew about Jake.

Shamus raised his eyebrows. "You got the complicated part right. What do you need for me to do?"

"Backup. I don't think Jake and Lilith are tied, but when Jake shows up, I'm worried Lilith might see it as a distraction and a lucky break for her."

Shamus nodded. "Lilith is definitely an opportunist. You and Justin take on Jake; in the meantime, Lilith is mine. Anything else?"

Wren's mouth quivered with a weak smile. "That's probably plenty for one day. I have a question about Lilith: does she always farm out her dirty work?"

"Only when she needs intimidation through brute force; I'm certain she killed Simone."

"She seems very calculating; what motivates her? Power? Money?"

"Money; I'm certain if she had a choice of power or money, she'd chose money every time. You can always buy power if you have the money."

"Is Desirada in danger?"

Shamus side-glanced Wren. "Desirada is always in danger, but she's a chameleon. You never see her unless she wants you to see her. Have you noticed?"

Wren furrowed her brow. "Rascal always sees her before I do."

Shamus chuckled. "She's always been a softy when it comes to dogs or cats."

Wren tilted her head as she peered at Shamus. "Are you from here?"

"Technically, no; I was born and raised upriver, as they say, but this was my area in my professional life. Gilly and I spend most of our time now on the road. When we find somewhere we like, we stay a spell."

"Really? Where were you before here?"

"We spent the last four months in Wyoming. I'd heard it was a great place for camping and perfect for stargazing. We'd still be there, but I must have swamp water running through my veins because I missed it. What about you?"

Wren told him about the travel magazine and where she'd been.

"Haunted campgrounds sound like something Gilly and I would love; we'll have to check them out. Do you expect Justin to text you before he arrives?"

"He probably will."

Shamus pulled a business card out of his pocket. "Text me if he does or whenever you need us in place; so Gilly and I can wander back to the dog park. It's not a bad spot to stand watch over the campground, except for the cabins."

Wren glanced at the business card and smiled at the child-like drawing of a truck and trailer with a stick man and a stick dog standing next to it and a phone number at the bottom. "This is a perfect business card."

Shamus grinned. "My talented granddaughter drew it for me when she was four; she's grown now, but she told me it was a picture of me when I got old because I'd always have a dog. My daughter saved the drawing and surprised me with the cards when I retired."

After Wren and Rascal returned to the trailer, Wren refilled Rascal's water bowl, and he took a long drink while she unfolded the papers that were almost dry.

Wren furrowed her brow. *I'd forgotten about Penelope; I should have asked Shamus if there was a connection between Penelope and Lilith.*

Wren's phone rang. She smiled and quickly poured herself a glass of iced tea while she answered Betsy's call.

"I won't keep you long, but I overheard Sheridan tell Socorro that Cody was in Colorado. Don't tell anybody, but Cody must have a girlfriend because Sheridan said something about a girl named Deb."

"I don't think..."

Betsy interrupted. "I don't think I've ever heard anyone mention Deb, either. Do we need to worry about Cody and a gold digger? He's young, attractive, and has a well-paying job; at least, I think he does because lawyers make a lot of money, don't they?"

"I'm sure..."

"You're right, but what I really called you about is I got a phone call from Jake. She wanted to know where Justin was staying tonight because she needed to talk to him, and his phone must be off. I told her he was on assignment, so I really didn't know. She got a little snippy and asked why he would have an assignment in Louisiana. Isn't that the oddest thing you've ever heard? I didn't care for her attitude, so I didn't even mention that she was confused because you're in Louisiana; instead, I told her she obviously knew more than I did, and she hung up on me. Was that the wrong thing to say?"

"Absolutely not; it's none of Jake's business where I am. I appreciate it. She's being a pest when it comes to Justin, and he's too kind to say anything."

"My thoughts exactly. Are you doing okay? How's the novel coming?"

"Rascal and I are fine; I finished the last article for the travel magazine, so the novel is my focus now."

"That's great; we got a larger than usual delivery of items for the store, so I have restocking that needs to be done. It was nice talking to you." Betsy hung up.

"That was an interesting tidbit, Rascal."

Rascal opened his eyes and stared at Wren when she mentioned his name.

"Jake called Betsy to ask where he's staying tonight. Betsy did a great job of irritating Jake because Jake hung up on her." Wren smiled.

Rascal sighed and closed his eyes.

Wren's phone rang, and she immediately picked up Justin's call.

"We're about thirty minutes away. Did Pat call you?"

"Yes, and I talked to Naomi after she and Jake had an argument, and Jake left in a huff. Naomi isn't sure whether Jake will return."

"I think she will. I talked to the RV dealership in Mobile, and they mentioned you had called to ask which campground I was going to, and they told you, or her, actually. Pat and I aren't sure how she knew I flew from Tucson to Mobile. He's going to ask around to see whether anyone in the office may have casually mentioned it in the grocery store or at the gas station."

"The good news is that no one can blame Betsy; Jake called her today and asked where you were staying tonight. Betsy told her you were on assignment. When Jake asked her why you were on assignment in Louisiana, Betsy didn't like the way Jake talked, so she told Jake that she obviously knew more than Betsy did. Jake hung up on Betsy."

Justin chuckled. "Remind me to tell Betsy she's a rock star."

Wren rolled her eyes. "She'd faint if you did that. Armand sent us backup. I'll introduce you to Shamus and Gilly when you get here."

"Shamus and Gilly are our backups?"

Justin was quiet for a few seconds while the sheriff spoke.

"The sheriff said we had the best. See you soon, sweetheart."

After they hung up, Wren sent Shamus a text. "J is 30 min away."

Shamus replied, "Going to the dog park in 20."

"Justin's going to be here in thirty minutes, Rascal. I'm really excited. We can sit outside to watch for him, but I'll pace. Can I drag you back to the registration office?"

Rascal moaned; when Wren opened the door, he slowly made his way down the stairs.

"You don't have to go if it's going to be that painful, Rascal."

Rascal flopped down next to Wren's camping chair; Wren strolled to the office.

When she went inside, Naomi narrowed her eyes then smiled.

*Naomi must be under a lot of strain; her smile is pretty forced.*

"You're getting to be my regular; what can I help you find?"

Wren smiled. "I'm being nosy because I'm bored. Did you hear from your cabin person?"

Naomi snorted. "I'm actually glad you stopped by because I don't have anyone else to talk to about that entitled lowlife. She called and ordered me to go to her cabin to pick up her things. Can you believe that?"

Wren raised her eyebrows. "Ordered you? Who does she think she is?"

"Exactly; I told her I would never go inside someone's cabin alone. I felt like she was setting me up so she could accuse me of stealing money or something. Is that paranoid?"

"From what you've said, I don't think so. Her request is really bizarre; she either wants her things or she doesn't, but I don't understand why she thinks it would be your responsibility to pack up her belongings and practically hand-deliver them to her."

"Thank you; I told her I was locking up and leaving because it was actually past closing time, anyway. If you can believe it, she screamed I was obligated to stay, so I hung up on her."

"That's horrible. Don't let me stop you unless there is something I can do to help you." Wren headed to the door.

"I'm fine. I already closed out the register, so I'll be right behind you. The drop box for cabin keys is clearly marked, but if she doesn't drop them off, I'll have the lock changed."

As Wren strolled back toward the trailer, she heard Naomi close and lock the office door. Wren turned and waved as Naomi drove toward the driveway.

After she returned to the trailer, Wren sat in her camping chair and scratched Rascal's ears.

"You won't believe what Jake told Naomi on the phone, Rascal; Jake is really losing it."

A soft breeze blew Wren's hair into her face; as she brushed it away, she glanced at the wispy clouds in the sky and listened to the call of a nearby mourning dove.

"I'll be right back, Rascal. I need my hat to keep my hair out of my eyes."

She went inside, twisted her hair on top of her head, and put on her Cranky Crawfish ball cap. When she returned to her chair, she glimpsed Shamus and Gilly on their way to the dog park.

When she heard a car as it came down the driveway toward the office, she frowned. *It's a little early for Justin.*

Her eyes widened when she recognized Naomi's car. Naomi drove past the office and continued toward the cabins. A few minutes later, Naomi left the campground a second time.

"That was strange, Rascal. Do you think she left a note for Jake?"

Wren rose from her chair and strolled a few feet away from the trailer toward the path that led to the cabins behind the row of campsites.

She returned to her camping chair and sighed. "I'd love to read the note Naomi left, but it's too risky. I've been nosy enough for today."

Wren peered at her phone. "Any time now, Rascal."

Wren listened to the raucous cry of a crow as it flew overhead then the repertoire of a nearby mockingbird. When she heard the crunch of tires on the gravel driveway, Wren rose from her chair to get a better look.

When she saw the sheriff's cruiser, she squealed, and Rascal yipped. Justin hopped out of the car the second it stopped. Wren ran to him, and he lifted her off her feet in a bear hug. She wrapped her arms around his neck and lifted her chin, and he kissed her.

He set her down, but kept his left arm tightly wrapped around her shoulders. The sheriff came around the cruiser with Justin's backpack; after he set it on the picnic table, the two men shook hands.

"Thanks for the encouragement, Vic; I had no idea how much I would learn at the conference, and it was a real bonus to find a network of my peers."

"I appreciated your company; if you hadn't agreed to go, I might have stayed back because of the investigation, and the panel for smaller regions with fewer resources would have been scrapped. That would have been an unrecoverable loss to the association. Stay in touch."

The sheriff climbed back into his cruiser but stopped at the dog park on his way to the exit. After a brief conversation with Shamus, he left.

Justin held Wren, and she wrapped her arms around his waist.

He exhaled. "Let's go inside, so I can change into a T-shirt then we can sit outside, relax, and talk."

After the three of them went into the trailer, Justin pulled off his collared knit shirt. Wren's eyes widened and her pulse quickened at the sight of his rippling muscles.

Her knees felt weak, so she sat on the sofa. She sighed in disappointment as he hurried to the bedroom to put on a T-shirt.

Rascal jumped up next to her, and she hugged him.

"Did you know how gorgeous he was, Rascal?" Wren whispered.

"Did you say something, honey?" Justin asked as he joined them in the living area.

Wren felt her face warm. "I was talking to Rascal."

"Oh, secrets?"

"Not from you; we'll talk about that later. I need to catch you up on everything I know about Jake."

"Inside or outside?"

"Outside; if Jake doesn't show up soon, we are going to the Cranky Crawfish for a celebratory dinner."

"What are we celebrating?"

"Being together."

Justin pulled Wren to her feet and put his arms around her. "Before we go outside, can we have a celebratory kiss without a campground audience?"

Wren tipped up her chin as he leaned down and nibbled her lip then kissed her sweetly; he leaned back and met her gaze. As she smiled and pulled him close, he kissed her open mouth with building passion. Wren matched his longing in a toe-curling kiss.

When they reluctantly broke away, Justin nuzzled her neck and groaned, "I love you so much, babe."

Wren hugged him. "This is how it's supposed to be; I love you."

They clung to each other until Rascal whined.

"Sorry, Rascal," Wren said. "Honey, we need to go outside..."

Justin's eyes twinkled as he interrupted her. "For a cool down?"

Wren sighed. "Probably, but's a good thing we have Shamus for backup because I'm a mess of emotions right now."

As she sashayed to the door, Justin whistled.

Wren put a hand on her hip and glanced over her shoulder with her best imitation of a sultry look. "Flattery will get you everywhere, my man."

"We'll continue this conversation later, sweet thing, and that's a promise." Justin massaged her shoulders then followed her outside.

# Chapter Twelve

When Wren stepped outside, she instantly went on alert. She glanced at Justin. *He's all business. We're ready, Jake.*

"Is it possible that Jake returned while we were inside the trailer?" Justin asked.

"We have a simple answer; let's take Rascal to the dog park."

Rascal dashed ahead as Wren and Justin strolled hand in hand to the dog park.

When Rascal reached the gate, Shamus opened it for him; Gilly pounced into the play position, and when Rascal yipped, she grinned and raced away into her zoomies.

Justin reached out his hand. "I'm Justin."

Shamus smiled as they shook. "Shamus. No one has come into the campground since the sheriff left."

"Good." Wren told the two men what Naomi had told her about Jake. "The original spat between Naomi and Jake started when Jake found a voodoo doll on her porch; Naomi dismissed it as something a feral cat must have dropped off. A little later, Jake claimed she found a dead rat in her cabin. Naomi immediately checked and found nothing, so Naomi must have been convinced Jake was trying to pull off some kind of scheme."

"On the surface, Jake sounds like a nut case." Shamus furrowed his brow as he rubbed his chin.

"She'll be here," Justin said. "It won't be dark for another hour, but I'm not sure she'll wait until after dark, though, if the rat incident actually scared her; of course, there's always the option that she was being dramatic for effect."

"We're going to relax a bit in front of our trailer, Shamus; we'd like to go to the Cranky Crawfish for dinner," Wren said.

"That works for us," Shamus said. "When you leave, Gilly and I will go into our trailer; she can sleep, and I'll have a perfectly comfortable perch to keep an eye out for cars entering the campground. I'll text you if anyone arrives and doesn't immediately go to a trailer."

As Wren, Justin, and Rascal left the dog park, Wren said, "I'll show you an alternate trail to the cabins from here; it's wide enough for golf carts but not cars."

"Is it the trail where we came across the alligator?" Justin asked.

"No, this is a smaller, ungroomed trail that goes around the perimeter of the campsites. It's more of a service road for the staff golf cart, so they have a way to get around the campground without having to share the road with cars, trucks, and RVs."

Wren and Justin walked past the firepit to a lane with grooves from the golf cart tires and a mound of overgrown grass and weeds in between the tracks; Rascal investigated the surrounding area but stayed close to them.

When they rounded a slight curve, Justin said, "I see the cabin." Wren said, "There are actually four cabins, but they're set back from each other, so that each cabin has the feel of being alone in the woods. You can see only the first one from the restrooms."

"That's really nice; what about driving to the cabins?"

"The service road goes behind the cabins. The driving lane to the cabins ends at the fourth cabin. I'll show you."

"How did you know all this?" Justin asked.

"Rascal and I did a little exploring right after you left for your conference."

Justin exhaled. "I thought you were going to stay away from the trail."

"We did; this isn't the alligator trail."

Justin muttered, "You don't know that."

"Are you mumbling at me? Rascal would have told me if there was an alligator ahead of us, just like he did on the trail."

"There has to be something wrong with your logic; I'll get back to you when I figure it out," Justin grumbled.

Wren rolled her eyes. "I'll be waiting."

"Good."

Wren giggled as they continued their walk.

"What's so funny?" Justin asked.

"I can't really say because you went for the last word, so if I say anything you didn't win."

He chuckled. "And don't you forget it."

When Wren stopped, Justin and Rascal stopped too.

"I have more to tell you about the rat; I didn't want to say anything in front of Shamus," she said. "There's a ghost..."

Justin interrupted, "I've been meaning to ask you about a ghost."

"The ghost is the young girl, Mara."

Justin nodded. "Julia Brown's daughter."

Wren told Justin about Mara and the dead rat.

He shook his head as he chuckled. "Sounds like you have an ally."

Wren smiled. "I know, but I feel a little guilty. Am I a bad influence?"

Justin hugged her. "Yes, sweetheart, you are."

Wren swatted his arm. "Thanks for always being there for me."

Justin kissed her. "Any time."

Wren sighed as they continued their walk. "I love you even when you're a terrible tease."

"I know."

When they neared the cabin, Justin grabbed Wren's arm. "Honey, there's a trail camera pointed at the cabin. Let's go back the way we came."

"Wow, I didn't see it. I thought Naomi was leaving a note for Jake."

"I didn't see any cameras near the other cabins, but I'd like to double check, just in case," Justin said.

After they reached the fire pit, Justin said, "I didn't find any other cameras; Do you think Naomi wants a record of when Jake returns for her belongings?"

"Seems a little extreme to me for someone who fills in at the campground only occasionally," Wren said.

"Could the camera be something Babette used?" Justin asked as they continued to the trailer.

"I could ask Armand, but is it important?"

"I guess not."

While Justin folded up Wren's camping chair and put it away, Wren and Rascal went inside.

After Wren fed Rascal, her phone buzzed a text from Shamus.

"Car came in and drove toward cabins. Justin walked past the restrooms. Need backup?"

"Yes. Rascal and I will circle around back."

"Gotcha."

"Let's go, Rascal, but you'll have to be quiet."

Wren and Rascal raced to the service trail and continued past the farthest cabin from the restrooms then slowed as they crept toward Jake's cabin.

Wren paused when she heard Jake's voice; after she pulled out her pistol from its holster, she held it at a low ready position and slowly continued with Rascal at her side.

"You've fooled everyone but me, Marshal." Jake's tone was patronizing. "You're not as smart as everyone thinks. I'm the only one who really cares about your success; you need my help."

"We might have different views," Justin said.

Wren peered around the curve and slowly continued moving until she saw Justin who stood in a shooting stance next to the front of Jake's car with his pistol drawn.

When Wren moved to see Jake, Justin's eyelashes flickered, and she stopped when she saw Jake's extended hands that held her pistol pointed at Justin.

Wren's eyes widened. Mara was ten feet away from Jake. She grinned at Wren as she swung a dead rat by its tail.

Jake sniffed. "Something stinks."

Justin sniffed. "Smells like something dead; must be a dead rat."

"Don't say that," Jake shrieked.

"Dead animals bother you?" Justin asked.

"I don't like rats," Jake growled.

"If you'll set down your gun, I could dispose of it for you," Justin said.

"I'm in charge here, not you," she shouted.

"On the count of three," Wren whispered.

Mara grinned; Rascal stepped in front of Wren, and Justin tapped his left foot three times.

Wren continued to whisper, "One, two, three."

On three, Rascal snarled, Mara tossed the dead rat, and two shots rang out.

Mara danced with her hands over her head, and Rascal barked then returned to Wren.

"That was amazing, Wren. You called in all the backup, didn't you?" Justin lowered his gun and stepped away from the car toward the cabin.

Wren re-holstered her gun as she fought her rising panic. "I heard two shots; were you hit?"

"I'm fine, honey; thanks to you, Rascal, Mara, and the dead rat."

Wren rushed to Justin then turned toward the cabin. Jake was on the ground on her back with a growing red stain on the left side of her shirt and a dead rat near her face.

A truck roared down the lane from the restrooms toward the cabin. Wren waved at Shamus, who slowed then stopped his truck. He lowered his window. "The sheriff's on the way; do we need an ambulance?"

Justin knelt next to Jake and felt for a carotid pulse. "Nope, but they can continue if they're on the way."

Mara stood next to the rat; after she picked it up by its tail, Mara swung it over her head and flung it into the woods.

Justin laughed. "Well done, Mara."

Mara curtsied then disappeared; Wren smiled.

"Do you need me to stick around, Justin?" Shamus asked.

"I'm fine. I'll wait for the sheriff; take Wren and Rascal with you, if you don't mind."

"Wren? Care to catch a ride home?" Shamus asked.

"Is that what you want? Are you sure, Justin?" she asked.

"I'm positive."

"We'd love a ride, Shamus," Wren said.

After Wren opened the back door of the pickup, Rascal hopped in with Gilly who was wagging her tail and wiggling her bottom so fast that she fell off the seat.

On the way to her trailer, Shamus said, "I'm getting old; I could have sworn I saw a dead rat fly into the woods."

"Shadows do funny things, don't they?" Wren asked.

Shamus side-glanced at her. "I have a feeling they frequently do when you're around."

When Shamus stopped at her trailer, Wren climbed out; Gilly whined after Wren opened the back door, and Rascal hopped out. Wren snatched up Gilly who was poised to jump out with Rascal.

"Sorry, Gilly, but we'll see you tomorrow." Wren placed Gilly on the back seat.

Gilly flopped down and glared at Wren.

"I'm in trouble, Shamus." Wren closed the door.

"We think you're probably used to it. We'll talk later, right?"

"Right; not everything is settled quite yet, is it?"

"Unfortunately, no." Shamus raised the windows of his truck then headed toward his trailer.

After Wren and Rascal were inside the trailer, she heard a siren on the road that stopped before it reached the campground. She watched from the window as the sheriff's cruiser roared down the driveway toward the restrooms. A few minutes later, an ambulance followed a deputy's cruiser past the restrooms.

"I hope Justin isn't too long," Wren said. "I'm looking forward to a dinner date with him. Should I dress up, Rascal? Maybe put on a clean shirt?"

Rascal closed his eyes.

"I'll take that as a yes." Wren hurried to the bedroom to check for a shirt that was dressy enough for a Friday night dinner date.

She pulled out a green shirt that buttoned down the front and held it up while she considered it. *Mom got me this shirt; it's supposed to be the same color as my eyes.*

"I wonder if Justin will notice," she mumbled as she buttoned it.

She stood in front of the mirror and examined the shirt. She had left the top button unbuttoned because that's what she always did.

Wren wrinkled her nose. "I look a little uptight."

She unbuttoned the second button. "There, that looks better: dressy, but casual."

When Justin came into the trailer, he whistled long and low. "You are gorgeous, sweetheart. That shirt is…"

Justin grabbed her in a hug and kissed her neck. "Definitely enticing."

She giggled. "That tickles and sends shivers down my back."

"I owe you a celebratory dinner; give me one second to change my shirt."

While Justin changed, he said, "I have to hear more about those shivers. We're going to the Cranky Crawfish for our celebratory dinner, right?"

"Yes."

After he came out of the bedroom, he said, "I had one clean dress shirt left. Have I told you that you are the prettiest girl I've ever seen?"

Wren put her nose in the air and walked prissily to the door then fluttered her eyelashes at Justin.

"You're even gorgeous when you're acting goofy, babe," Justin said.

Wren giggled as she picked up her backpack. "I'm ready."

On the way to the Cranky Crawfish, Justin said, "Jake found the trail camera and smashed it. Vic was a little sad that there was no video of what happened, but he said my statement was thorough, so they didn't really need it. I left out the part when a ghost smacked Jake on the side of her face with a dead rat."

"She did? Mara really has remarkable aim."

"I couldn't see her, but when I saw the dead rat, I knew it was Mara. The dead rat and Rascal's ferocious growl definitely threw off Jake's aim. Vic and I think her shot went high into the trees and to my left. I was waiting for her next to her car, but I didn't expect her to step out with her gun pulled. She probably glanced out the window before she came out. In hindsight, I should have stayed hidden until she came out of the cabin and remained behind the car, but it all worked out despite my poor judgment. It was interesting that I could hear you so clearly, and Jake, or should I say Deb, did not. Your voice sounded like it was carried by the breeze coming from the trees."

"I took a chance that you would be tuned to my voice, and she would be so focused on you she wouldn't hear me. When she didn't react when I said on the count of three, I knew we had her."

"I was worried about what I would do until I heard you; I was on alert, and the distractions were perfect."

"When you told Mara thank you, she curtsied."

"She did? Thank you for telling me." Justin exhaled. "The next time an irate citizen or council member gets in my face, I'll remember that Mara acknowledged my thank you with a curtsy."

Justin squeezed Wren's hand and chuckled. "Of course, I could always call for distractions."

Wren giggled. "I can't see Thomas tossing dead rats."

"He'll enjoy your stories about the ghosts you've met. Did you know you've taught me that people-watching is very educational?"

Wren leaned back, closed her eyes, and listened as Justin talked about the different styles of the people who were at the conference.

Justin interrupted himself. "We're here. The parking lot is packed."

"Go around to the back; not very many people think about parking there because it isn't paved."

When Justin turned to go to the back, he chuckled. "It's all trucks back here."

"We're supposed to go inside through the back door. We'll be seated family style with the locals."

"Isn't that like boarding house style where you sit at a large table with a bunch of other people?"

"It sounded like it to me; what do you want to do? We can always go around front."

"Did you see the line? It was outside the door. Haven't you been treated like a local since you got here, and everywhere you've been now that I think about it? No sense breaking tradition." Justin parked. "I'll get your door, sweetie; I want to spoil you as much as I can."

On the way to the door, Wren said, "I forgot to tell you I bought a dozen cookies here earlier today; just in case somebody mentions cookies."

"Were they good?"

"I only had one, and it was delicious."

"Then that's my story; you ate all the cookies and didn't share." Justin opened the back door to the restaurant for Wren and grinned.

"You're incorrigible." Wren elbowed him as she went past him.

Justin leaned down and whispered, "I love it when you talk dirty."

Wren glared at him and snorted to cover up her growing smile. "You are too full of yourself and having too much fun."

When they were seated at a large table with four other people, everyone introduced themselves by first and last names and who their kin was. When it was Wren's turn, she said, "I'm Wren…"

The woman next to her interrupted. "Wren, honey, we know who you are and your pen name. We're looking forward to reading your article about the Cypress Knees Campground. We're pleased to meet you and Justin and thrilled you chose Mahoneville for your honeymoon."

Wren felt her face warm; she glanced at Justin, who beamed.

"Speaking of the Cypress Knees Campground, did you hear what happened there earlier?" an older woman at the end of the table asked. "One of the state troopers tracked down a serial killer and shot and killed him at the campground. The killer was fixing to go on a spree in the bayou, but thanks to the skills of our Louisiana State Police, we're safe."

"Where'd you hear that?" The man next to her asked.

"At the gas station while you was inside paying," she said.

"Have you ever written any true crime books, Wren?" the first woman asked.

"No, I write for a travel magazine, so there isn't much call for true crime stories."

"Justin, I understand you attended the conference in New Orleans. Did you meet my brother, Roland Guidry?" the man across from him asked.

"The name sounds familiar; I must have," Justin said.

The man nodded. "Knew you would."

The server set glasses of sweet tea in front of Wren and Justin. "Okay folks, the special tonight is crawfish etouffee; if anyone would rather have something else, you're welcome to join the line out front and order off the main menu and get yourself a nice slab of meatloaf with instant mashed taters and fresh sweet corn straight outta the can."

Everyone laughed.

While a bus girl set two large pitchers of sweet tea on the table, the server continued, "Y'all enjoy your meal this evening, and don't worry about saving no room for dessert because you always swear you will but never do. We'll send you home with your dessert in a paper box for your midnight snack or breakfast in the morning."

Wren leaned close to Justin and whispered, "I'm going to the restroom to see what is on the main menu."

When Wren rose, the woman across from her rose too. "Are you going to the ladies' room, Wren? I'll go with you."

Wren glanced at Justin who winked at her. She rolled her eyes. *I'll hear about this later.*

Wren started toward the front, but the woman said, "No, this way, honey."

As the woman led her to a restroom near the back door, she said, "My mama always told me men thought ladies went to the restroom in pairs because it was safer, but my mama said the truth was that it was the only way to catch up on the latest gossip."

Wren raised her eyebrows. "So, what's the latest gossip?"

Wren and the woman went into the anteroom with soft chairs, pale green walls, and fresh flowers in a vase. The woman motioned toward the chairs. When she sat, Wren sat too.

"You catch on quick, girl. Penelope was supposed to be all broken up about Simone's death, but the arguments those two had weren't your typical old lady banter. There was bad blood there."

"I didn't realize that," Wren said.

The woman nodded. "Penelope went into seclusion because she was embarrassed that everyone knew how shabbily she treated her sister. I think she's suffering from remorse, which is a little late, from my point of view. You might hear rumors she killed Simone, but that's not true at all. You look real hard at whoever tells you that because they're part of Lilith's circle."

Wren gazed at the woman's face. "Really?"

"More than likely; either that or an idle airhead that repeats whatever nonsense they hear; watch yourself either way. Shall we wash our hands?"

After they left the restroom and were on their way back to the table, Wren said, "Thank you so much for the company. I always thought going to the restroom in pairs was an old-fashioned custom."

"Oh, it is, but that doesn't keep it from being useful, does it?" the woman smiled.

"Not at all." Wren returned her smile.

When Wren returned, Justin rose and held her chair for her as he raised his eyebrows.

Wren whispered, "Later."

The server and two helpers swooped to their table with large trays of food; Wren gaped at the large serving of crawfish etouffee over rice when a server's helper placed an oversized bowl in front of her.

The woman next to her smiled. "It's enough to feed a family of four, isn't it? No one but a farm hand could eat all this food; they'll box it up for you. It's even more delicious as a leftover."

The server placed large bowls of hush puppies, baked beans, potato salad, and bread baskets of French bread on the table to pass around. "Enjoy!"

Wren smiled as Justin and the man next to him, who was a long-time trapper, got into an animated discussion about trapping coyotes.

"The man's version of going to the restroom," the woman across from Wren leaned forward to avoid being overheard.

Wren chuckled and nodded.

While she ate, Wren watched an animated conversation complete with waving forks used as punctuation at the end of the table. Justin rested his arm across her back while he leaned close. "I can't understand what they're talking about, but it's definitely entertaining."

Wren turned to whisper her reply, but accidentally brushed his chin with her lips, so she kissed his cheek.

Wren giggled. "That was fun."

"No fair; I was ambushed." Justin squeezed her shoulder then leaned back and was pulled into a new conversation about road conditions.

After everyone had eaten their fill, the server asked, "Who's ready for dessert?" She cackled at the groans while her helpers handed out to-go boxes for the diners' leftovers and white plastic bags with the pre-packaged desserts inside the bags.

It took half an hour for everyone to go through the nice-to-see-you conversations and to shake Justin's hand and hug Wren as they congratulated them on their recent nuptials.

# Chapter Thirteen

After they were on their way to the campground, Wren said, "I feel bad that I didn't set Desirada straight that first night when she said we were on our honeymoon."

"It's not like we're trying to steal their money, sweetie. A man told me tonight it was refreshing to see a young couple that had been together as long as we have get along so well."

"What? How long did he think we'd been together?"

Justin shrugged. "I don't know."

Wren narrowed her eyes. "Yes, you do; what did you tell him? How long?"

"I told him I've known you practically forever, which is true because my world turned upside down the minute I saw you in the coffee shop."

Wren sighed. "That was such a sweet thing to say; I felt the same."

"That is good, so tell me about the menu or whatever you learned when you left the table."

"I learned women always go together to the restroom to share the latest gossip, and I was reminded about someone we'd forgotten all about." Wren told him what the woman said about Penelope, including the admonition to be wary of anyone who insinuated that Penelope had murdered Simone.

"That's huge; what do you think? Do you believe what she said?" Justin asked.

"It made complete sense to me that Lilith would take advantage of Penelope's guilt and blame her for Simone's murder. I was thinking earlier that everyone had forgotten about Penelope, so I can see where the people who loved to be in the know would seize onto the idea that Penelope murdered her sister."

Justin nodded his head. "Did the woman have any idea who Lilith is?"

"If she did, I don't think she'd admit it even to herself. Lilith has the reputation for being ruthless."

"Here's a twist for you," Justin said. "Do you suppose Penelope might have an idea who Lilith is or has the same information as Simone?"

Wren furrowed her brow. "How do I find Penelope?"

"Me and my big mouth," Justin grumbled. "Hand it off to Armand."

Wren nodded.

"Did it bother you when you heard a state trooper caught up with a serial killer at the campground?" Wren asked.

"Not one bit; I'd much rather be under the radar than a local celebrity with Lilith running around. I'm worried enough about you becoming a target as it is."

After Justin parked in front of the trailer, the man in the trailer across from them waved as he came outside with a trash sack in his hand. When Justin opened Wren's door, the man stopped near the back of the truck.

"Y'all missed a bit of excitement here. The place was crawling with state troopers after one of them found a serial killer who was one of the state's most wanted. The trooper got the drop on the killer; I heard the trooper had a flesh wound but will be fine. Did you go out to eat?"

"We went to the Cranky Crawfish; the food was excellent."

"I heard about them earlier; maybe I'll take the missus out for dinner tomorrow night to give her a break from cooking."

"Food's good; if you like Cajun food, don't order off the menu. Tell them you want the special," Justin said.

"We can't eat anything spicy, so we might have to read the menu to be sure we understand what we're ordering."

Justin nodded. "Makes sense to me."

Wren opened the trailer door, and Rascal hopped out.

As the man headed toward the dumpster, Justin shook his head.

"You tried, honey," Wren said.

"I'm sure the meatloaf will be fine for them. I'll put our leftovers in the refrigerator, then we can go to the dog park," Justin said.

As they strolled toward the brightly lit dog park, Shamus and Gilly came out of their trailer. Rascal yipped, then he and Gilly raced to the dog park.

Gilly slid into Rascal in her excitement; Rascal bumped the gate, and it opened. Gilly raced around the perimeter while Rascal investigated a small section of grass.

Shamus chuckled. "I guess somebody didn't latch the gate when they left; how was dinner?"

Wren told him about the family style table.

"I'd heard they'd established a new menu for the tourists, but I didn't realize they'd kept the old recipes for the locals."

Wren furrowed her brow. "Shamus, is Penelope safe?"

Shamus sat on the bench. "We're not sure; she was staying with someone she trusted, but she slipped out last night, and no one knows why or where she went."

"What's your theory?" Wren asked.

Shamus rose and rinsed the dog bowl then refilled it from the faucet.

After he returned to the bench, he gazed at the sky. "No stars; guess we'll get us a little rain tonight."

Wren side-glanced at Justin who nodded.

"Do you think Penelope has a dry place to stay?" Wren asked.

Shamus exhaled and narrowed his eyes as he turned his gaze toward Wren. "I don't know if you're a bulldog that won't let go, or a Pomeranian who is nipping at my heels."

Justin laughed. "Sorry, honey, but he's right; face it, Shamus, you can't shake her."

"Penelope is not a young woman; she would have found a safe place to stay before she left," Shamus said.

"Good; can we talk to her?" Wren asked.

"We?" Shamus chuckled.

Justin shook his head. "Careful Shamus, it's a trap."

"Wren, where would you go if you were Penelope?" Shamus asked.

"I'd have three choices: Simone's, Desirada's, or Babette's house because I don't know anyone else."

"Those are too obvious; where would be less obvious?"

Wren smiled. "Right. Got it."

"You got it?" Justin asked.

"I think she does," Shamus said. "My work here is done."

"That's right, thanks. Let's go, Rascal." Wren headed toward the gate.

Justin reached the gate before Wren did and opened it. "I guess we're leaving, Shamus; thanks for the help, I think."

On the way back to the trailer, Justin asked, "What's your plan for the rest of the evening, honey?"

"I have some loose ends that I've been ignoring because I was so focused on Jake."

"Me too." Justin put his arm around Wren. "We need to talk."

"I agree completely; I'm positive I have all the right pieces to find Penelope, or maybe even stop Lilith."

"Like the pieces of paper next to the stove?"

"Right. Did they look dry to you?"

"They were pretty close."

"Those are the papers Babette had hidden in her socks. I don't know what is on the papers because I had to wait for them to dry before I could pull them apart, but they might still be illegible."

"Let's see what they say."

After they were inside the trailer, Justin put the dried, stuck papers on the table and frowned. "Pulling them apart would tear the paper."

"We could try to slip something thin in between the pages, but a knife would cut the paper, so that won't work."

"I might have just the thing in my tool kit; I'll be right back," Justin said. Wren examined one set of papers. "I see numbers on this top page."

She copied the numbers into her notebook, then examined the other. "Here's a name: Jeremiah Boudreaux."

When Justin returned, he showed Wren a long, thin, smooth piece of metal. "This is a Slim Jim; it unlocks vehicles with horizontal and vertical linkages. In fact..."

Justin glanced at Wren as she rolled her eyes then cleared his throat. "If you're interested in its history or how a Slim Jim works, you can look it up, but it might be thin enough to separate the papers. Will I be forgiven if it doesn't work?"

Wren smiled. "Of course, but before you start, do you see anything here?" Wren pointed to the first page.

"They're pretty faint, but I see numbers; looks like maybe six digits." Justin squinted as he read the numbers aloud.

Wren checked her notes. "That's what I thought too. Now, look at this one."

"I see a name." Justin furrowed his brow. "Jeremiah Boudreaux; is that what you saw? Do you know him?"

"Boudreaux is probably a common name; that's Naomi's last name. Do you see anything else?"

"That's it."

"Same for me; give your Slim Jim a try."

Wren put her hand on her chest and sighed at Justin's intense concentration. *He is so dreamy; I adore his determination to be successful.*

After Justin uncovered the next page, he exhaled. "Here's something: Coastal Landsavers, Inc."

"Seriously? Let me show you something." Wren showed Justin the newspaper classifieds that list Coastal Landsavers, Inc. as the buyer of five foreclosed properties in one week.

Justin narrowed his eyes. "Who are the officers of Coastal Landsavers?"

Wren searched the internet. "I don't find any record of Coastal Landsavers, Inc. in Louisiana. They could be incorporated anywhere." Wren furrowed her brow.

Justin narrowed his eyes. "What are you thinking?"

"Gage has all kinds of contacts."

Wren sent a text to Gage. "Who are the officers of Coastal Landsavers, Inc.? They are buying foreclosed property in Louisiana, but I don't think they're incorporated in Louisiana."

Gage responded, "On it."

Wren showed her phone to Justin.

Justin chuckled. "You've made lifelong friends, haven't you?" Justin cleared his throat. "Speaking of which..."

Justin's phone rang; he sighed, then answered. "Is everything okay, Pat?"

Justin nodded as he listened. "Just a second."

Justin lowered his phone. "Pat has a couple of things for me; I won't be long."

"Go ahead; I'd like to write until bedtime."

Wren set up her laptop and smiled. "My novel needs a little pizazz; time to stir it up."

After two hours, she stretched and smiled. Justin was asleep in his recliner, and Rascal was curled up in her recliner.

She set up the coffee for the next morning.

"Honey?"

Justin jumped then smiled. "I must have fallen asleep."

"If you and Rascal would go outside for a break, I'll get ready for bed and pull out the sofa, then we can all go to sleep for the night."

Justin yawned. "Did you get much writing done?"

"Quite a bit."

When Justin and Rascal returned, Wren was in her pajamas and had set up her bed for the night.

Justin hugged her, and she lifted her face. After a sweet kiss, Justin said, "We need to talk tomorrow; I love you."

"I love you too."

# Chapter Fourteen

The gurgling coffee woke Wren; she inhaled its rich, comforting aroma that enveloped her with its cozy sense of warmth. *Just like Justin.*

When she stretched, Justin said, "If you'd like to take your shower now, the coffee will be the right temperature for you by the time you're dressed."

"You always wake up before I do," Wren mumbled as she grabbed clean clothes and stumbled to the bathroom.

When she got out of the shower, her stomach rumbled when she smelled bacon. *There's nothing like the bacon to start a day off right.* She quickly dressed and brushed her hair.

When she came down the steps, Justin pointed to the table. "There's your coffee. Do you want your egg scrambled?"

Wren giggled as she picked up her cup. "Surprise me."

"Good answer." Justin smiled.

After they ate breakfast, Wren took over the dishes and straightening the kitchen while Justin checked his emails.

After she converted her bed back to the sofa, she picked up her dirty clothes. When she picked up her jeans, the ring she'd found earlier fell out of her pocket. She examined it. *Maybe this is Naomi's. I'll ask her.* She stuck it into her pocket. "Rascal and I are going to inspect the campground."

Justin nodded.

After they were outside, Wren glanced at the registration office. "Naomi's car is parked in front; I can see if the ring is hers or Babette's and ask her if she knows Jeremiah Boudreaux."

Rascal flopped down next to the trailer steps.

Wren shrugged as she headed toward the office; before she reached the building, Rascal raced past her and waited next to the door.

"Thanks, Rascal; I won't be long."

When Wren opened the door, Rascal stood in the doorway while he softly growled.

"I can't close the door with you in the way, Rascal," Wren said.

Rascal continued his low growl.

Wren shrugged and went inside; Naomi wasn't standing in her usual spot behind the desk.

"Naomi?"

Wren waited a few seconds then stepped closer to the partially opened storage room door. "Naomi?"

Rascal's growl turned to a snarl.

When Wren turned around to leave, she saw Naomi lying on her back behind the desk.

"Naomi, are you okay?" Wren rushed to her but stopped at the sight of Naomi's open, lifeless eyes, the deep, red gash across her throat, and the large butcher knife in the middle of her stilled chest.

Wren grabbed onto the counter to keep from falling; while she screamed, Rascal snarled and barked. She ran out the door with Rascal at her side as she raced to the trailer.

"Justin!" she cried out as she opened the trailer door and stumbled into Justin's arms.

"What's wrong, honey?" Justin held onto her to keep her from falling.

Wren sobbed. "Naomi's in the office; she's dead."

"Dead?" Justin's back stiffened.

Wren's panicky voice rose in pitch as the words tumbled out. "Someone slashed her throat and left a big knife in the middle of her chest."

"Shh; I've got you." Justin stroked Wren's hair away from her face as he helped her to the sofa.

"Stay right here, sweetheart," he whispered.

Justin slammed the door as he raced out; Rascal jumped onto the sofa next to Wren and leaned against her.

She sniffled as she tried to regain her composure. "Thank you, Rascal. It was such a shock seeing Naomi."

Wren wrapped her arms around Rascal and buried her face in his neck. "I thought she was Lilith, but I was wrong."

When Justin returned to the trailer, he rushed to Wren and put his arm around her as he joined her on the sofa. "The sheriff would like to ask you a few questions; if you don't feel up to talking about what you saw, I'll tell him now is not a good time."

"I'll help as much as I can."

Justin sent a text and received a reply almost immediately.

"Okay, the sheriff will be here shortly."

Wren giggled.

"Are you okay, honey?"

Wren sniffled. "Sorry; I'm sure I'm not thinking straight, but did you just call me shortly?"

Justin stared at her then laughed. "You are absolutely unpredictable; are you telling me I said he'll be here, shortly?"

Wren nodded as she smiled.

Justin shook his head. "How do you do that, sweetheart? I'm worried sick about you, and finding Naomi like that must have been a horrible shock, but you still make me laugh."

"I'm glad you understood what I meant; someone once told me I wasn't as funny as I thought."

"Someone has no appreciation for your unique, brilliant sense of humor."

Rascal yipped; Justin opened the door. "Come on in, Vic."

Justin motioned toward the recliners as he returned to sit next to Wren.

After the sheriff sat down, he pulled out a small notebook from his shirt pocket. "Tell me what you saw, Wren; take your time."

When Wren swallowed hard, Justin put his arm around her and gently patted her shoulder for encouragement.

Wren exhaled. "Rascal and I went outside for his break; I went to the office to say hello to Naomi."

"Any particular reason?" Vic asked.

"Naomi was in the office, and I had another question about local history."

Justin furrowed his brow as he glanced at Wren.

"Tell me what happened; I'll try not to interrupt," the sheriff said.

After Wren described what she saw after she went inside, Vic asked, "Could anyone have been hiding while you were inside the building?"

"I don't think so, but the storage room door was partially open; when I peeked inside, I didn't see anyone."

"Sorry if you've already told me, and I missed it, but how did you know she was in the office?" Vic asked.

Wren tilted her head as she peered at the sheriff. "I thought I told you her car was parked in front of the building."

"Was Naomi's car there when you went to the office, Justin?"

"Sure was."

Vic frowned. "It wasn't there when I arrived."

Wren shuddered; Justin's grip on her tightened.

"Are you going to be okay?" Justin whispered as Vic pulled out his radio and stepped outside.

Wren stroked Rascal's neck. "Rascal stood in the doorway and growled when I went inside."

Justin exhaled. "If Naomi's killer was hiding, Rascal made him think twice about attacking you. I took a quick look at Naomi and called the sheriff as I left; if the killer was still there, he knew he had only a few minutes to escape."

Wren furrowed her brow then gazed at Justin. "How did the killer get to the office? Why did he take her car?"

Justin met her gaze; they said in unison, "The bayou."

When Justin opened the trailer door, Rascal hopped out.

"The sheriff's gone," he said.

"Let's check to see if there's a boat at the landing," Wren said.

When they reached the boat that was pulled up and tied to a pole, Justin said, "This must be the killer's boat; I'll call the sheriff."

"Give me a second; I'll check with Armand to see what he suggests."

Justin peered over her shoulder as Wren sent the text. "Poisonous catfish. Can you advise?"

"Poisonous catfish?" he asked.

"I'm not sure if there is a poisonous type, but catfish are known as bottom feeders; he'll understand."

Wren's phone rang.

"What's going on?" Armand asked.

"I have you on speakerphone, so Justin can hear. Naomi was murdered, and her killer took her car. Justin and I found a boat at the campground landing."

"How long ago was she murdered?"

"Not more than half an hour ago; we think the murderer was hiding in the storage closet when I found her. Rascal probably saved me from being attacked."

"Think you could head up the bayou in that boat you found?" Armand asked.

"If it has enough gas, sure." Wren stepped into the boat, unscrewed the cap, and peered inside. "Looks like it has plenty."

"No," Justin said.

Armand added, "Justin, we'll need you to meet us at the Cranky Crawfish to pick up Wren. I'll meet her on her way up the channel, and we'll ditch the killer's boat before we continue to the restaurant."

Justin glared at Wren, who returned his glare.

"Rascal goes with Wren," he growled.

"It's the only way to do it; Wren, text or call if you run into any problems." Armand hung up.

"I hate this whole thing." Justin untied the boat after Rascal hopped in.

Wren put on the lone life vest before she started the motor and waved to Justin. "See you at the Cranky Crawfish."

Justin scowled as he stood on the bank with his arms crossed.

When Wren turned her attention to the channel, Rascal had his front paws on the seat at the bow.

"Stay low, Rascal; it will be easier for me to see and give you a chance to get your sea legs." She maneuvered the boat to the middle of the channel.

After they rounded the first bend, Wren said, "This is very similar to the small boat the course instructor used for our training. I'm glad I had a chance to study how Armand maneuvered the bayou. Justin wasn't exactly thrilled, was he?"

Wren continued up the channel. "Armand went a little faster when I rode with him, but I learned a lot from him."

When she rounded a bend in the river, she said, "We should be coming to the cabin where Armand talked to the young woman."

Wren exhaled as she saw the cabin. "It's nice to know we aren't lost, Rascal."

After the cabin was behind them, Wren said, "I was a little disappointed we didn't see the mother and her baby, but I guess it's just as well; we don't want the rumor getting around that we were cruising the bayou."

Wren heard a boat engine heading toward them from up river. She cut back her engine and sent a text to Armand. "Goldfish. I think you're close."

He responded, "If you just passed the cabin, yes. Pull close to the bank but don't get yourself stuck."

Wren exhaled. "Okay."

When Armand reached her, he slowed. "Good job, Wren; you're a natural. After I turn around, follow me. We'll ditch the boat."

Armand led her into a narrow channel. "Do you think you could get it into those weeds up there on the right?"

Wren nodded.

"Come up next to me, so I can help Rascal into my boat, then we'll pick you up."

Wren slowly eased the boat next to Armand.

"Okay, Rascal, go." Wren motioned toward Armand's boat, and Rascal hopped over.

"That was a slick move, Rascal; well done," Armand said. "Your turn, Wren."

Wren opened the throttle and rammed the boat into the weeds. When it lurched to a sudden stop, she laughed. "That was fun."

Armand pulled close to the stern and held out a life vest. "Take off that vest and put on this one."

After Wren changed life vests, he held out his hand. "Your turn."

Wren stepped into Armand's boat.

On the way to the Cranky Crawfish, she asked, "Why did we steal the boat?"

Armand chuckled. "We didn't steal it; we only moved it. Lilith must have been using it to get around the bayou. She's getting sloppy because we're getting close, and losing her boat will agitate her even more. Send Justin a text; ask him to park at the far end of the Cranky Crawfish parking lot then meet you and Rascal at the boat landing. Order their breakfast special or coffee and a beignet, and eat at a picnic table on the porch. Enough people will see you, so there's no way Lilith would think you had anything to do with the boat disappearing."

After Wren sent the text to Justin, he replied.

Wren said, "He'll be there in ten minutes."

"I knew he'd speed to get there. We'll get there a few minutes before he does, so you can wait for him near where he'll park, and I'll be somewhere fishing."

"Do you know where Penelope is?" Wren asked.

"She's safe; why?"

"I think she knows why Simone was killed."

Armand nodded. "You're probably right, but the tricky part is proving it."

"Do you know whether Penelope has any proof?"

"No, but Lilith must think she does."

"Have you heard of Coastal Landsavers Investment, Inc.?"

Armand frowned. "I don't believe I have; why?"

"At one time, they were buying up quite a bit of foreclosed property in the area; I think they still are. What about Jeremiah Boudreaux? Is he a relative of Naomi's?"

"Jeremiah Boudreaux? I don't recognize the name. We might need to check with the older crowd though, if you're trying to trace Naomi's relatives. Any reason why?"

"I'm not sure; he might be part of the Coastal Landsavers Investment, but I don't really know."

"I'll be seeing some old-timers later; Naomi's name will definitely come up. I'll ask about her relatives. Do you think there's a tie to Lilith?" Armand asked.

"I don't know; there could be, but right now, I'm convinced everyone has a tie to Lilith except for you, Babette, and Shamus. One more thing, is there any significance to a ring with a large pearl-like stone?"

Armand stared at Wren. "You described the Tante Julie Brown's ring; it's a legend and doesn't exist. How did you know about it?"

"What if it existed?" Wren peered at Armand.

Armand shook his head. "I don't even know; do I need to find out?"

Wren searched his serious face. "That would be nice."

Armand slowed down as he neared the Cranky Crawfish. "My head's still messed up over the ring. I need a little time. If you have it or you've seen it, Wren, nobody can know."

Armand exhaled. "What about Naomi? Did she have a tie to Lilith?"

Wren furrowed her brow. "I think she did; she must have outlived her usefulness." Wren shuddered. "Bad choice of words."

After Wren and Rascal exited the boat, Armand said, "I had another thought, Wren. When you get your beignets, put them in your backpack; you want to look like you've been sitting there a while. After a couple of people see you, leave since you've been there such a long time."

Wren smiled. "Will do; thanks."

Wren and Rascal reached the parking lot and met Justin after he backed into a parking spot away from the front of the café.

Justin put his arm around Wren as they hurried to the front porch. "What now?"

"I'll go inside and put in an order for beignets and coffee while you and Rascal sit at a picnic table. I'll join you and explain everything."

When Wren walked inside, the young cashier asked, "Are you here for breakfast, Miss Wren?"

"We have Rascal, so we'd like to sit at a picnic table. I need two coffees and a large sack of beignets."

"I'll be right behind you, with cups and a carafe of coffee."

The cashier followed Wren outside.

Justin was sitting at the picnic table that was closest to the wooden bear. He smiled. "Rascal wanted to sit here."

The cashier giggled as she poured their coffee. "I'll have those beignets in a jiff; I'll bring you a treat, Rascal."

When the cashier returned, she said, "I brought you plates and napkins to go with your bag of beignets. Rascal, chef carved the bone out of a beef steak for you. He said cooked bones splintered too easily; I didn't know that."

After the cashier went inside, Wren put a beignet on each of their plates. When she took a bite of hers, powdered sugar dusted her shirt. She brushed at it and looked down. "That's better."

She wrapped her beignet in a napkin and dropped it into the sack.

Justin took a large bite of his beignet before he pulled it apart into two halves and put a half on each of their plates. "I assume it's okay if we eat the evidence."

Wren giggled as she put the sack into her backpack and set it down next to her.

She picked up her beignet. "Cheers."

"I learned a Cajun toast this week." Justin bit his lip then tapped her pastry with his. "To love, laughter, and happily ever after."

Wren felt her face warm; she smiled. "I like the sound of that."

Justin exhaled. "Good; we still need to talk."

Wren nodded. "Right; I owe you an explanation. Armand wanted the boat gone to irritate Lilith. He thinks she's getting sloppy."

"He might be right."

Wren leaned toward Justin and lowered her voice. "We're supposed to look like we've been sitting here a while, so no one gets the idea we had anything to do with the boat. When someone brings up Naomi's death today, Armand will ask about her family; he'd never heard of Jeremiah Boudreaux. Oh, and Penelope is safe, but she doesn't have any proof why Lilith killed Simone. It sounds like everybody knows Lilith killed Simone, but there's no proof."

Justin glanced at a truck that pulled into the parking lot. "We look too serious; let's talk about when we want to leave."

Wren inhaled. "The swamp smell reaches the Cranky Crawfish restaurant; wouldn't you expect it to chase off nonlocals?"

"Maybe that's part of its charm." Justin patted her hand.

"It definitely adds to the Louisiana ambiance. I'd like to stay for tonight's music unless you want to leave earlier," Wren said.

Justin smiled. "Did we decide whether our plan for our first day of travel is to see how far we can go, or will we pick a campground where we'll stop?"

Wren giggled. "I want to do both, but why don't we see how far we can get before we decide what we want to do the next day?"

Justin peered at her. "I have absolutely no idea why that couldn't be a great idea, but I'm positive any plans we make will suddenly change at the last minute."

Wren nodded. "It does seem to be the way we operate, doesn't it? I have a little more to talk about, but it's serious, so I'll wait until after we leave."

Wren poured the rest of the coffee from their carafe into their cups. "Drink up, cowboy."

"You got it, babe; them cattle rustlers ain't going to catch themselves."

Wren laughed as two locals headed toward the café.

Justin smiled. "We've been here most of the morning; you feel like loading up the mules and packing out, darlin'?"

"I love it when you talk that cowboy lingo." Wren smiled as she gazed at Justin.

"You two leaving so soon?" Remy, the accordion player, stopped before he opened the door.

"Excuse me," the other local side-stepped Remy and went inside.

"We're planning on first thing in the morning," Justin said. "We don't want to miss the music tonight."

"Appreciate your support." Remy went into the café.

"There's our two," Wren said. "You ready to leave?"

After Justin left a tip under the napkin holder on the table, they strolled to the pickup.

Justin started the engine. "Where to from here?"

"Back to the campground; I'm torn between stopping Lilith and getting out of here."

"You don't have a patent on that, sweetie. I'm starting to realize what you've been through since you left Hidden Gulch. Has it been like this at every campground?"

"You want the polite answer or the truth?" Wren asked.

"Why don't we chalk it up to a rhetorical question?"

She nodded. "We can talk about it much, much later."

Justin glanced at her. "We need to talk."

"You're right; is after we get back to the trailer okay?"

"Something like that."

When they returned to the trailer, Wren said, "I found a ring in the storage room."

Wren removed the ring from her pocket and showed it to Justin.

Justin gaped at the ring. "Wow; this is a gigantic stone; it looks like a pearl. What is it?"

"I don't know; Armand said it might have belonged to Aunt Julie Brown."

Justin searched Wren's face. "Mara would know, honey; why don't you take a picture of it?"

Wren snapped the photo. "You're right about Mara; I'll ask her."

After Wren sat on the sofa, Justin joined her and put his arm around her. "Do you know how to find her or contact her?"

Wren shook her head. "She'll be at the fire tonight; the only other times I've ever seen her is when I needed help."

Justin groaned. "That's not comforting."

"Sorry; since we're leaving tomorrow, I'd like to do the laundry before we leave. Can you think of anything else?"

"Are you sure we shouldn't leave today after lunch?" Justin rose and began pacing.

"I can't take the ring with me. If it belonged to Tante Julie Brown, shouldn't it stay with Mara?"

"Who would Mara want to have the ring?" Justin asked.

"I don't know, but I would think Babette," Wren said.

Justin rubbed his forehead. "What if we left right after the music ended this evening?"

Wren rose and stepped in his way to block him; she giggled when he took the hint and hugged her.

She wrapped her arms around him and snuggled against his chest before she looked up to gaze at him. "I don't mind traveling at night, but we should let people know we're leaving."

"You're talking about Mara, Desirada, and Armand, so he can tell Babette, right?"

Wren nodded. "Yes, and you'd want to tell the sheriff."

Justin exhaled as he released her and resumed pacing. "I'm so conflicted; other than how much I appreciated being invited to attend the conference, the only thing I have to tell the sheriff is that my sweetie stole a boat."

Wren snorted as she flipped her hair. "According to Armand, I did not steal a boat; I merely relocated it for safekeeping and to irritate Lilith."

"That's not how it works," Justin said.

"If Lilith files charges against me, I'm sure Cody will find me an appropriate Louisiana lawyer to defend me."

Justin stopped pacing and laughed. "Fair enough; we'll wait for Lilith to file charges."

"If we're leaving tomorrow, I'd like to catch up on the laundry this morning."

"Before you go, I'd like to plan meals for a few days. While you're doing laundry, I'll shop for groceries."

"I already have a list of what we're low on." Wren opened the drawer closest to the door, pulled out a sheet of paper she had folded in half, and handed it to Justin. "I saw the butter pecan ice cream, so we're set for dessert; we have to remember we have it, so we can eat it."

"Add it to your list of things for us to do." Justin chuckled as he read the list. "This is fairly complete, honey."

"We have enough beignets for breakfast for at least three days; can you pick up an airtight container?"

"Will do; I'll carry the laundry basket for you then I'll leave for the store."

# Chapter Fifteen

When Wren, Justin, and Rascal went outside, Shamus and Gilly were headed toward their trailer. Shamus unclipped Gilly's leash; when Rascal yipped, Gilly raced to greet him.

While Rascal trotted around the trailer, Gilly zoomed past him as she rounded each corner at her frenetic pace.

Shamus smiled. "Gilly and I thought we'd hit the road today, but I got a call from Babette's mother. Babette is doing much better, but Mrs. Dupre asked me to hang around to keep an eye on the campground until next Saturday when Babette will return to work. Gilly and I put up a sign on the office door for instructions on how to check in online; thank goodness Mrs. Dupre can take care of that. Gilly and I will make sure everyone's safe and the campground is clean."

"I'm happy to hear Babette is doing better." Wren said.

"It's great news, isn't it?" Shamus continued, "Desirada came by my camper before daylight this morning and gave me this old photo to give to you, Wren. It's from the early 1900s.

Desirada said Julie Brown called the young woman her niece, even though they technically weren't related."

When Shamus handed the faded photo to Wren, Justin peered over her shoulder. "Wren, she looks a lot like you."

Shamus nodded. "That's what Desirada said."

Wren turned over the picture; the faded writing on the back was in pencil. "1914. Sparrow."

"Sparrow?" Justin asked.

"Amazing coincidence, isn't it?" Shamus asked. "Desirada said to tell you that Julie Brown's best friend, Phoebe, was from Georgia, and her daughter was Sparrow. This photo was taken the last time Phoebe and Sparrow visited Julie Brown."

"Wow. I'll have to ask Mom about Phoebe and Sparrow." Wren snapped a picture of the old photo.

As Wren and Justin strolled to the laundry room, Rascal raced ahead.

After Justin set down the laundry basket in front of a washer, he kissed Wren. "I won't be long."

Wren started the washer then sent her snapshot of Sparrow's photo to her mom.

A few minutes later, Wren's phone rang. *Mom's fast.*

"Hi, honey, the picture looked exactly like you, so at first I thought you'd gone to one of those old-fashioned photographers and had your picture taken. I was shocked when I read your text that said the girl in the picture was Sparrow and was taken in 1912. My great-grandmother's name was Sparrow, and her mother was Phoebe. That's about all I can remember other than a few fanciful stories my grandmother told me about Phoebe and Sparrow and their trips to Louisiana; I'll have to dig into the old family records to see what else I can learn, but what an interesting find. How did you come by the photo?"

Wren told her about Julie Brown. "I was told her best friend was named Phoebe, and Sparrow was Phoebe's daughter."

"Isn't that something?"

"I'll mail the original photo to you as soon as I have a chance."

"That's so exciting; let me know if you learn anything else."

"That's all I know about Phoebe and Sparrow, but I have more information about Julie Brown that I'll send to you."

After they hung up, Wren sent a text to Justin. "Mom said her great-grandmother's name was Sparrow."

Justin immediately called her. "Wow, that's really amazing, isn't it?"

"She told me she has a friend who is really into genealogy; sounds like Mom will pick up a new hobby. I may end up with more fresh stories."

"I'm almost finished at the grocery store; see you soon."

When Wren's phone rang almost immediately after they hung up, she smiled. *He thought of one more thing.*

Her eyes widened when she realized it was Armand calling.

When she answered, Armand said, "I gotta be quick. The ring originally was Julie Brown's and was supposed to be the source of her strength. It's been passed down over the years; Simone had it for safekeeping. Lilith killed Simone because she wanted the ring, but Naomi found it first and stole it. I'm convinced we have a leak somewhere. Hide the ring; don't let nobody know you have it. So far, Lilith thinks I do. One more thing: I don't know if it's important, but my daddy told me Remy is an old-time nickname for Jeremy."

Armand hung up.

"Where can I hide the ring, Rascal?"

Wren glanced around the trailer. "I've got an idea."

She wrapped the ring in aluminum foil then put it into a small, clear storage bag; she waded up two more pieces of foil about the same size as the foil with the ring, then stuck one piece in each of her front pockets.

"Let's go outside, Rascal." Wren strolled around to the back of the fifth wheel and inspected the water pressure, the electrical connections, and dropped the plastic sack with the ring into the open end of the pipe on the back of the fifth wheel where the sewer hose rode during transport; she secured the dangling cover on the end of the pipe. Wren returned to the front of the trailer and sat at the picnic table and scanned the surrounding campsites. She scratched a hole under the table in the sandy dirt with her heel.

"Nobody's watching, right, Rascal?" she mumbled. She casually pulled out a piece of foil and dropped it on the ground then pushed dirt over it with the heel of her boot when she stretched and glanced around.

"Ready for a romp at the dog park?" Wren smiled as Rascal yipped.

As Wren walked to the dog park behind Rascal, she imagined eyes watching her from every RV and trailer window. She pulled out a dog pickup bag from the dispenser with a flourish and wandered around the park while Rascal investigated the perimeter. When he stopped for a bio break, Wren waited then scooped up the poop with the dog bag.

She glanced around with the most suspicious style she could muster before she dropped the last bit of wadded up aluminum foil into the doggy bag. She knotted the bag then strolled to the waste disposal can and dropped in her knotted bag. After she brushed her hands together in a semblance of satisfaction, she sighed then sat on the bench until Rascal trotted to the dog park gate.

Wren smiled then sauntered toward the trailer while Rascal trotted in front of her.

After they were inside the trailer, Wren leaned against the door. *Showtime's over, folks.*

Wren collapsed on the sofa, and Rascal jumped up with her. Wren exhaled. "Did I go overboard, Rascal? I hope I drew some attention away from Armand. Lilith can't be everywhere, but I'm convinced she's here or will be."

Rascal laid his head on her knee, and she rubbed his ears.

When Wren heard a vehicle pull in and stop in front of the trailer, she whispered, "Is it Justin, Rascal?"

Rascal grinned, and Wren relaxed.

"Thanks," she whispered as she hurried to unlock the door and open it.

"I might have gone overboard, but we won't starve." Justin stood outside the door holding eight sacks of groceries.

Wren gaped at the sacks. "Can I help you?"

"Nope." Justin struggled to walk up the steps then maneuvered sideways to get through the door with his load.

When he set all the sacks on the counter, he grunted, "Got it."

As Wren began emptying the sacks and putting away food, she said, "You could have brought in the groceries with two trips."

"What?" Justin poured a cup of coffee then set it into the microwave to heat it. "Why would I want to do that?"

Wren rolled her eyes. "Maybe it would have been safer?"

Justin snorted. "I was fine."

While Wren folded the sacks for reuse, Justin gazed at the sky. "According to the local weather, we might have rain later, but the sky's clear for now."

"Armand called me." Wren told him what Armand said. "I wrapped the ring in aluminum foil and put it in a plastic sandwich bag before I stuck it into the sewer storage tube." She told him about the shallow hole next to the picnic table and the dog pickup bag.

Justin paced while Wren talked; he stopped and stared at her when she explained her diversion with the dog pickup bag.

After he resumed pacing, he said, "A leak makes sense; Armand has done a great job of drawing away attention from you, but the leak may be watching us. I haven't seen any security cameras other than that one trail camera, have you?"

"Babette told me there weren't any security cameras. According to the bad guys, there was an undercover cop, and Naomi told me Jake claimed to be undercover, so maybe Naomi kept track of Jake with the trail camera."

Justin stopped. "Could the bad guys have meant me?"

Wren shook her head. "No, everybody knows you're a marshal, so you're not undercover at all."

Justin crossed his arms. "Is the ring the only reason we can't leave? Why don't we give the ring to the sheriff?"

Wren glared at him as she rose and headed to the door. "I need to check with Mara."

"We can't leave without the permission of a girl who is a ghost?" Justin growled.

Wren stormed out and slammed the door.

After she stomped away from the trailer, Rascal joined her at the firepit; Wren stopped and glanced behind her. Justin had paused ten yards behind her as he casually scanned the sky.

Wren kept her head down as she hurried to where he stood. She put her arms around him, and he hugged her.

"Sorry," they said in unison.

"I don't know why, but it's important to you that the right person has the ring. Am I close?" Justin asked.

"Yes, and I don't know why it's so important either, but..." Wren exhaled.

"It is." Justin finished her sentence.

She nodded. "Thank you."

"Where were you going?" Justin asked.

"I want to see if Desirada is home."

"Let's go, then."

As they held hands and strolled to Desirada's trailer, Wren side-glanced at Justin. "Does this mean I owe you one unreasonable decision without pouting or throwing a fit?"

Justin chuckled. "I'm side-stepping that trap; I won't admit I'm ever unreasonable, or that you would ever pout or have a tantrum."

Wren giggled. "You are so smart."

When they reached Desirada's home, Wren lightly tapped on the door, and it swung open. "Desirada?" Wren called out.

"Hush, girl," Desirada whispered. "Come on in."

After the three of them were inside, Justin quietly closed the door behind them.

Desirada came from the back of the trailer. "I figured the best place to hide was to keep moving from one obvious place to the next. We can sit down."

Desirada sat on the broken-down sofa, and Wren sat next to her.

When Desirada raised her eyebrows at Justin, Wren said, "He paces."

Justin nodded; Rascal flopped down in front of the small kitchen sink.

Desirada nodded. "A good man who thinks on his feet. Why are you here, sha?"

"I need to talk to Mara."

Desirada peered at Wren. "So talk to Mara."

Wren glanced toward Rascal as his wagging tail thumped on the vinyl floor. Mara stood next to him.

"Mara, I have a ring that may have belonged to Julie Brown; who do I give it to?"

Mara smiled as she pointed to Wren.

Wren furrowed her brow. "It's not mine; it's yours, Mara."

Mara rolled her eyes.

Wren laughed. "You're being sassy, aren't you?"

Mara smiled and nodded then raised her eyebrows at Desirada.

"Tante Julie Brown gave the ring to her best friend's daughter, Sparrow. The ring is yours, Wren," Desirada said.

"I thought the ring should stay here; shouldn't we give it to Babette?"

Mara shook her head.

"Can I give it to my mother, Mara? Her full name is Carolina Wren, and she heard stories about Sparrow when she was growing up. It would mean a lot to her."

Mara raised her hands over her head and danced in a circle.

"Good; that's what I'll do."

After Mara finished her dance, Wren narrowed her eyes. "Mara, I have to stop Lilith, don't I?"

Mara's expression instantly changed as she furrowed her brow and slowly nodded.

"Who is Lilith? Where can I find her?"

Mara stared at Desirada.

Desirada sighed. "Lilith always moves from one obvious place to another, and that includes the firepit."

Justin's eyes narrowed as he placed his right hand on the butt of his gun on his right hip. "Mara, is Desirada Lilith?"

Desirada jerked her head and peered at Justin.

Mara grinned and shook her head.

"Justin, Mara said, no."

Desirada laughed. "Wren, you gotta love a man who covers all the bases."

"You're right, Desirada."

"Thanks, Mara," Justin said. "I hope there are no hard feelings, Desirada."

"Not at all; you're looking out after your wife. You're a good man, Marshal."

Wren cleared her throat. "Desirada..." she glanced at Mara who shook her head. "Our best chance to stop Lilith is to go to the firepit tonight, isn't it?"

Desirada said, "I'm sorry to say you are right; take backup."

Wren rose. "We'll do that; will you be there?"

"Absolutely; I want a front-row seat when you take down Lilith, but don't expect an attack until after the music ends and everyone clears out except for you, your backup, Mara, and me."

On the way back to the trailer, Justin said, "I thought you were going to say something to Desirada about, you know, but you asked about Lilith and the firepit instead."

"Mara shook her head."

Justin smiled. "I like Mara. Did I miss anything else?"

"You missed Mara's dance when I asked if I could give the ring to my mother."

"So, she said no to Babette; did she want the ring to go to your family because her mother gave it to Sparrow?"

"That was my understanding; Mom will love it."

"Are you ready for lunch?" Justin asked. "I'm starving."

While they ate, Justin said, "Speaking of starving..."

"Which was a half hour ago," Wren giggled.

Justin raised his eyebrows. "Do we want to save our leftover crawfish etouffee for the road tomorrow night and have dinner at the Cranky Crawfish tonight?"

"That's a brilliant idea."

"Why don't we take the afternoon off from your world of crime and go for a ride? There's a dog park about an hour away."

"That would be fun," Wren said. "I'd like to sweep and mop the camper floor and wipe down the counters before we leave. I'll be finished in about thirty minutes."

"Rascal and I will get out of your way and go fill up the truck."

"Perfect."

After Wren finished mopping, she sat at the picnic table to wait for Justin and Rascal and watched a hawk circle overhead. Two crows cawed in a nearby tree, and a squirrel joined in with its chatter.

*We'll need backup.* Wren sent a text to Armand. "Skulking pufferfish. Expecting L. at the firepit and need backup this evening. Shamus a good choice?"

"Yes. I'll be close too."

When Justin and Rascal returned, Wren said, "I checked with Armand. Shamus is a good choice for our backup, and he'll be around too."

"Let's go see Shamus, then."

"If we go to the dog park, Gilly will let him know."

Rascal yipped and raced to the dog park. Before Wren and Justin reached the park, Shamus and Gilly came out of their trailer.

While Rascal and Gilly played, Justin and Shamus paced the dog park. Justin told Shamus about the conference, then Shamus told Justin about some of his experiences.

Wren relaxed and listened to the birds. When her phone rang, she was startled. *I must have zoned out.* She answered as she strolled to the gate.

"When are you coming home, Wren?" Betsy asked.

Wren continued to walk a few feet away from the dog park to avoid interfering with the men's discussion. "We're leaving early tomorrow morning. We should be there no later than Thursday."

"That's perfect. Will you be too tired to go to Socorro's for dinner? Of course, you will, but you still have to eat, don't you? Are you going to stay at the campground? I already reserved your favorite spot for you, so you don't have to worry about not having a place to stay. What do you think you'd like for dinner? I'm trying to get Socorro to make tamales, so I might tell her tamales are your favorite, but I don't know what kind you like best."

"I love any kind of tamales, but I don't want Socorro to go to any trouble, and I'm not sure..."

Betsy snorted. "Don't be silly; we don't want to discourage Socorro from making tamales. Aaron and Natalie can't decide if they want to get married next year at spring break when the weather is nice or wait until the end of the school year. Butch says it's logical for them to wait until next year because this is Aaron's first year of teaching here, and he has a lot on his mind, but that's such a long time to wait. I guess that's how young people are these days; I don't understand where the fun is in being sensible, do you?"

Wren smiled. *Evidently not.* "I should tell you..."

"Sorry if I'm interrupting, but I have to tell you about my book club. I've been reading, and when Butch interrupts me, I tell him I have to finish the book because of my book club obligations. My book club of one has been very enjoyable. Butch says he's happy about the book club because I'm much more relaxed."

"That's perfect."

"I guess Cody and Deb didn't work out because he's already returned to Sedona. I'm actually relieved because we need to approve of his girlfriends before he gets too involved, don't we? I'll see you on Thursday; let me know if anything changes. Here comes Butch; he'll want his lunch." Betsy hung up.

While Wren strolled back to the dog park, she furrowed her brow. *Betsy assumed I'd be staying at the campground. I wonder what Justin is planning. We haven't talked about where I'll stay when we get to Hidden Gulch. I don't want to be at the campground without him, but he has a house. I wouldn't think he'd want to stay in the trailer. He keeps saying we need to talk; maybe this is what's been on his mind.*

When Wren crashed into the gate because she was so deep in thought, she jerked up her head to see if Justin had noticed and exhaled when she saw Justin and Shamus were walking away from her.

While Justin and Shamus talked, and Rascal and Gilly played, Wren sat on the bench and bit her lip as she stared at the ground.

*I thought I could stay at Justin's house, but he really hasn't invited me. Rascal and I would be happy at the trailer because I could write, and we could spend time with Betsy while Justin was working. We'd see Justin in the evenings.*

Wren rose from the bench and rolled her shoulders. *That idea stinks.*

She glanced at her phone. *It's too late to go anywhere, but Rascal and Justin are enjoying their afternoon.*

Wren inhaled the faint odor of the swamp and leaned against the fence while she watched the newest arrival of RVs and trailers as they crept to their assigned campsites. When the aroma switched from swamp to lighter fluid and charcoal, Shamus said, "It's getting to be about that time, isn't it? Where did the afternoon go?"

While Shamus called Gilly, Justin strode to Wren and put his arm around her. "I'm sorry, sweetheart; I promised you a long ride to get away from the campground, but Shamus and I were talking shop, and I lost track of time."

"We'll be on the road for the next few days, so I didn't mind at all. You and Rascal had a pleasant afternoon, and I actually relaxed for the first time in ages."

Justin squeezed her shoulder and kissed her cheek. "You're amazing. What about dinner? Shall we feed Rascal then go to the Cranky Crawfish?"

"I'd love it."

After they reached the trailer, Wren fed Rascal.

Justin glanced around while Rascal ate. "The trailer looks nice; when you said you wanted to clean it before we left, I thought it looked fine."

"We don't exactly see things alike sometimes."

"No kidding."

When Wren grabbed her light jacket and her backpack, Rascal flopped down on his rug and closed his eyes.

After Justin locked the trailer, he opened the truck door for Wren then hopped in. On the way to the Cranky Crawfish, Wren's phone buzzed a text.

"It's from Cody." Wren read the text aloud. "Heard about Deb. Are you okay?"

"Tell him I said to butt out," Justin growled.

"Justin! That was not very nice; he's practicing his social skills."

"He can practice on somebody else," Justin muttered. "Okay, I'll practice my social skills. I'm sorry he irritates me so much when it comes to you. How's that?"

Wren rolled her eyes. "Pitiful."

"Pitiful sounds better than not very nice."

"It's like half a step up."

"I'm not having one of my best days today; have you noticed?" Justin sighed.

Wren responded to Cody's text. "I'm fine."

Cody replied, "I'm sure there's a story. Can't wait to hear it."

"What now?" Justin asked.

"He knows there's a story, and he can't wait to hear it."

"I'll tell him…" Justin cleared his throat and scanned the sky. "No clouds; maybe we won't get that evening rain after all."

"Excellent recovery, Marshal." Wren snickered.

"Thank you, ma'am. I'm pleased to oblige," he drawled.

Justin parked in the back. When they went inside, the man who talked trapping with Justin motioned for them to join him and his wife.

"Good to see you two again." The two men shook hands.

The man's wife said, "That's the last we'll hear from them for the rest of the night. Tonight's special is gumbo. When are y'all leaving for Arizona?"

"Tomorrow morning."

"So soon? You'll definitely be missed. We'll make sure you leave with plenty of gumbo to get you home."

More people joined their table. A young woman with long black hair and eyes who could have been Babette's twin sat next to Wren. "Heard you were leaving, Wren. Babette's my cousin; she's doing really well, thanks to you. The family has something for y'all." The young woman put a bright green gift sack on the table.

Wren peered into the sack; her eyes twinkled as she pulled out a thick cookbook.

The young woman continued, "We published all of Meemaw's recipes in one big cookbook last year. We named the book Chef's Rescue Book because Meemaw would give each newlywed couple a stack of her handwritten recipes; she guaranteed her recipes would rescue any frantic newlywed cook. You're more than welcome to share it with Justin, if he's your chief cook, by the way, because Meemaw always said any man that couldn't find his way around a stove wasn't worth putting his feet under her table."

Wren grinned. "Justin's a better cook than I am. Maybe this will even us out a bit."

"Little bit of competition there?" The young woman giggled as she nodded toward her husband who was in a deep conversation with the woman sitting next to him. "That one's mine, and we're the same."

"Is there an easy section?" Wren opened the cookbook.

The young woman leaned closer and whispered, "You won't find this tidbit in the book, but the easiest recipes are marked with a shrimp. The ones with a crawfish are the next step up, and the catfish recipes are the most advanced, but they aren't hard. You'll be ready for the catfish recipes in a couple of months."

Wren's eyes welled up. "I can't tell you how much this means to me; thank you so much."

"We're glad for you to have it. Honey, we've all been there."

When their server and two helpers appeared with gumbo, rice, potato salad, collard greens, and hush puppies, Wren returned her cookbook to the gift sack.

After her first bite, Wren said, "This is so good."

Babette's cousin said, "Drop a bite of potato salad in it."

"You aren't joking?" Wren stared at her.

"Just do it."

Wren scooped up the gumbo-soaked potato salad into one bite and ate it. "That is amazingly delicious."

"Well, you're officially Cajun now, sha," the woman across from Wren said.

When everyone had eaten their fill plus a little extra, the server announced, "Ready for praline brownies, y'all?"

Everyone groaned; the server chortled. "Never gets old."

The server gave Justin three large to-go sacks with sturdy handles. "Chef said y'all will need lots of gumbo to get you across that heathen Texas. Miss Wren is in charge of your praline brownies."

A helper gave Wren a box of desserts.

When they were in the truck riding home, Justin said, "Do you feel like we're related to these folks? They felt like family to me."

"Babette's cousin gave me Meemaw's recipes. I cried only a little."

"You're going to cook Cajun? That's outstanding."

"You are too; there are some more difficult recipes for you to tackle."

"Really? Is this the best day of our life, or what?"

Wren gazed at him. *Our life? That sounds wonderful.*

After they were in the trailer, Wren packaged the gumbo into meal-sized portions and put three meals in the freezer and the fourth in the refrigerator.

"We can have crawfish etouffee tomorrow night then gumbo the next night. You'll have the option of more gumbo Tuesday night or something different."

"We'll be traveling like royalty, won't we?" Justin asked.

Wren set the large box of praline brownies on the counter. "I'll set aside two brownies and freeze the rest."

When she opened the box, her eyes widened. "We should cut the brownies in half."

Justin peered over her shoulder. "I'll cut, and you can wrap."

After all the brownies, except for two halves, were cut, wrapped, and in the freezer, Wren smiled at the sound of a fiddle being tuned.

"Ready for some music, sha?" Justin kissed her smiling mouth. She pulled him closer for a sweet kiss.

When Wren leaned back to gaze at him, she said, "Let's do this."

# Chapter Sixteen

Justin carried their camping chairs to the fire pit; Rascal stayed close to Wren.

When they reached the firepit, Mara stood next to Simone's chair. She waved at Wren; Wren grinned and returned her wave.

"Mara?" Justin whispered.

Wren nodded.

Justin waved at Simone's chair, and Mara giggled.

"You made Mara happy, Justin; she knows you're trying."

Justin beamed as he held up a thumb.

Desirada sat next to Simone's chair, and Shamus stood near a tree in the shadows.

Wren tugged on Justin's shirt sleeve; when he leaned close, she kissed his cheek then whispered, "I'm sure Armand's close."

Justin turned to return her kiss. "Yep."

Al tuned his fiddle with his non-injured hand while Remy played a few chords as campers came close to the fire with their chairs.

"Scoot on in, y'all, and grab your ringside seats," Al said.

While the early campers moved in, Wren leaned toward Justin and whispered, "Armand told me Remy is the nickname for Jeremy."

"Jeremiah Boudreaux?" Justin furrowed his brow.

"I don't know, but isn't it possible?" Wren whispered.

Justin cleared his throat. "Honey, I should circulate and tell a few folks goodbye since we're leaving first thing tomorrow."

Wren nodded and turned her attention to the musicians.

Justin returned as the music started.

He nibbled on Wren's ear. "This part is fun." He sighed. "We're all set. Shamus will let Armand know."

Wren turned and kissed his cheek. "It would be nice if we were wrong, but we aren't. I can prove it."

Wren raised her eyebrows at Mara and pushed her hair away from her face while she pointed at Remy.

Mara slowly nodded.

Wren rubbed her forehead and pointed at Al; Mara shook her head.

Wren blew Mara a kiss; Mara grabbed the air like she was grabbing the kiss, popped the imaginary kiss on her cheek, and smiled.

Wren returned her smile.

"Remy?" Justin whispered.

"Yep," Wren said quietly.

After a three energetic songs, Al said, "Time for a story, and it's my turn. This is the story of the rougarou, the werewolf. The rougarou roams the bayou, howling, and looking for her next victim. The rougarou is wicked and ferocious, but..." Al looked at each camper, one by one, then slowly shook his head as he continued, "not too smart."

Al paused for effect. "When the moon is bright, like tonight," Al pointed to the moon, "the rougarou prowls the swamp. It snarls as it searches for animals to rip to shreds and eat, but it particularly stalks children to snatch, especially disobedient children who don't eat their vegetables or go to bed on time." Al paused.

An adult camper howled.

Al continued, "The rougarou goes door to door as it rattles doorknobs to go inside, but the rougarou is no match for the mighty mama. Mamas put a box outside the door with thirteen rocks inside the box. The rougarou's one weakness is counting, but the rougarou can count only to twelve." Al raised his eyebrows.

The adult camper howled a second time.

"Mama put thirteen rocks in the box, remember? When the rougarou gets to the thirteenth rock, it doesn't know what comes after twelve, so it starts over. The rougarou spends all night outside with the rocks as it counts to twelve, then starts over until the sun peeks over the horizon. The rougarou runs away from the bright sunlight, and all the children are safe. Your mama knows protection magic."

"Is that true, Daddy?" a boy asked.

"Must be; I know your mama keeps you safe."

Al nodded. "Another thing that scares away the rougarou is music, so let's scare away the rougarou."

Al and Remy played an energetic, bouncy Cajun tune, followed by a waltz and more Cajun tunes.

After the last song, Al said, "Good night all; thanks to those who contributed to our tip jar, and if you're moved to drop in a bill or two before you leave, we appreciate your support."

As the campers filed past the gumbo pot and dropped in their tips, Al and Remy put their instruments into their cases. After all the campers left, Al picked up his stool and violin. "Marshal, would you mind carrying the gumbo pot to my truck for me?"

Justin froze as he stared at Wren.

She smiled. "I'll wait right here for you, honey."

Justin swallowed hard; Wren elbowed him and rose. He sighed as he picked up the gumbo pot and followed Al.

After they were out of sight, Remy set down his accordion in its case. "Well, Miss Wren, finally."

Remy switched his tenor voice to a falsetto woman's voice. "You've taken up too much of my valuable time and energy. It's time for the sad tale of the dead journalist who was too nosy for her own good."

Remy rose with a pistol in his hand, but Wren had her pistol aimed.

"Drop it, Lilith," Wren said.

Remy sneered as he aimed his gun. "I'm a better shot than you are, girly."

Wren spit out a curse the Cajun chef had taught her, and Remy's eyes widened, and his hands shook.

Rascal snarled, and Mara tossed a live, deadly cottonmouth snake at Remy; the snake wrapped itself around Remy's gun hand.

Remy screamed and tried to shake off the snake from his hand. A shot rang out; Remy dropped.

Armand stepped out from his hidden position behind the trees. "I had a clear shot."

Justin raced to Wren, with Shamus and Al behind him. Desirada hurried from her trailer.

Justin grabbed Wren to keep her from falling when her knees buckled.

"That was one heck of a curse, and to top it off with a cottonmouth that suddenly appeared from nowhere when it flew through the air? I'll tell you, Wren, I was terrified," Armand said. "Then I remembered I was a good guy and took my shot."

Wren furrowed her brow. "Al, what about the band?"

"Don't you worry, Wren; my wife has filled in for Remy when he was working and couldn't make it. She'd be tickled to be a permanent band member."

Wren exhaled. "That's a relief."

"I'll take you to the trailer, honey," Justin said.

Wren smiled at Desirada and Mara. "Thank you for all your help; I'll never forget you."

Mara put her hand on her heart.

"I love you too, Mara." A tear slipped down Wren's face, and she choked back tears as Justin guided her back to the trailer.

After they were in the trailer, Justin helped Wren to the sofa. "How about a glass of wine, sweetheart? We can both be off duty."

"Right; off duty."

Justin handed Wren a glass of wine. "We need to talk."

Wren nodded.

"You first," Justin said.

Wren narrowed her eyes. "Are you sure you want...never mind. I'll start. Betsy told me she made a reservation for the fifth wheel at the campground, so I'll have a place to stay. Your turn, Marshal."

"Oh. Well, that would work."

Justin rose and began pacing.

"Sit down, Marshal," Wren growled.

Justin glanced at his recliner then sat next to Wren on the sofa. Wren scooted close to him, and he put his arm around her. Wren sighed. "That's better. My question is where am I going to stay in Hidden Gulch?"

"I thought we...didn't we agree? What do you want to do?"

Wren glared at him. "I want to stay with you. You have a house in Hidden Gulch, so we either stay at your house or in the trailer. We need to make it official. Is that in line with what you want?"

"Make it official? We need to talk," Justin said.

"Fine; are we getting married?"

Justin stared at Wren then rose and went to the bedroom.

Wren put her hand over her mouth. "I messed up, didn't I, Rascal? I pushed too hard. It was too soon. We'll go to Georgia. I'll rent a car and drive straight through. Wait. I don't want to leave my truck, but I'll have to give it to Justin so he can get home. I ruined everything." Tears slipped down Wren's face as she rose. "Let's go sleep in a cabin with the dead rats."

"Honey?" Justin returned from the bedroom. "Are you okay?"

"Sure, I'm fine; dead rats don't bother me."

"We can stay wherever you want." Justin wrapped his arm around Wren and guided her to the sofa. After they sat down, he said, "As long as you will marry me."

Justin opened a small box with an emerald ring inside. "This reminded me of you. Will you marry me?"

"Are you going to be this aggravating our entire lives? Of course, I'll marry you."

When Justin slipped the ring on her finger, Wren leaned against him. "When's the wedding?"

"I thought we'd contact our mothers, so we could be married next Saturday in front of the old saloon; our favorite ghost, Thomas, can be my best man."

Tears streamed down Wren's face. "I love it. I love you."

# Chapter Seventeen

## A Week Later

Wren glared at her reflection in the mirror as she tugged at the bodice of her wedding dress. "I hate this dress, Mom; did you and Ellie really pick this out two weeks ago? There's too much cleavage showing."

Carolina smiled as she brushed away an imaginary piece of lint from her daughter's shoulder then held out her hand as she admired Sparrow's ring. "Wren, I can't tell you how special this ring is to me. Thank you so much."

Wren smiled. "You're welcome, Mom."

Carolina continued, "Wren, your dress is lovely and fits you perfectly. Ellie and I knew flouncy or frilly wasn't right for you, so we went with a simple dress that lightly skims your curves. I love the silky, white fabric and its lacy overlay; your dress has an old-fashioned style that is all you. I'm not sure I would have selected western boots to wear with such a delicate dress, but they fit the saloon setting, and it is your wedding. You talk to her, Socorro."

Socorro snorted. "Toughen up, buttercup; we've got a wedding to pull off, and we don't need any stinkin' whiners. You won't freeze; let's go."

Wren scowled. "Fine for you to say, but your dress is practically a turtleneck."

"Y'all can continue this argument after I leave for Georgia; I'm here to get my daughter married, so let's do this," Carolina said.

Socorro elbowed Wren. "She's bossy; guess you better get hitched or she'll have to stick around."

Wren laughed.

Carolina rolled her eyes. "You certainly have a way with words, Socorro. Now, how do we get out to that old dilapidated building y'all are calling a saloon?"

"We'll take the golf cart," Socorro said.

When Socorro parked in front of the old saloon, Wren smiled at Justin who wore his dress uniform; he gaped at her.

"He's the most gorgeous man alive," she whispered.

Wren's dad offered her his arm as she stepped out of the golf cart. After Carolina hurried to her seat in the front row, Socorro and Betsy walked down the makeshift aisle of folded chairs on either side.

Her dad whispered, "Ready, honey?"

Wren exhaled. "Ready."

They walked toward Justin who gazed at Wren and beamed as he stood with his dad near the preacher. Wren smiled at

Thomas who stood at attention on top of the saloon with his shotgun; his hat was at his feet, and his hair was slicked back.

After Wren stood next to Justin, her dad joined her mom in their seats in the front row, and Justin took Wren's elbow.

"About time you got here, Bird Girl. We was gettin' a bad case of the nerves here a'waitin' on ya," Thomas said.

When the preacher said, "If anyone here objects..."

Thomas was poised with his shotgun ready as he narrowed his eyes and scanned the guests and the horizon.

Wren glanced up at Justin and giggled.

Justin whispered, "He takes his job of best man seriously."

Wren nodded.

Wren met Justin's gaze while the preacher droned on.

Justin exhaled when the preacher said, "I now pronounce you husband and wife."

Wren smiled. *He was holding his breath too.*

While Justin kissed Wren, Thomas whooped, and the small group applauded then hurried to congratulate the newlyweds.

Justin whispered, "Finally."

Next to read:

TAGGED BY DEATH

RILEY MALLOY MYSTERY, BOOK 1

Only Riley, vet tech and dog whisperer, can identify the serial killer. The obsessed killer stalks her; Riley must die.

Check for other Judith A. Barrett books to read!

BarrettBookShop.com

*Browse, shop, read, enjoy!*

**Subscribe and Save**

Join the eNewsletter mailing list and become the first to know about book specials and read unpublished stories and exciting news!

JudithABarrett.com/newsletter

# Subscribe and Save

Join the eNewsletter mailing list and become the first to know about book specials and read unpublished stories and exciting news!

Be a VIP Reader!

SUBSCRIBE to her Newsletter via her website

www.judithabarrett.com/newsletter

BROWSE, SHOP, READ, ENJOY!

Find all the Judith A. Barrett books and series in the Barrett Book Shop to find your next book to read!

www.barrettbookshop.com

# More About the Author

Judith A. Barrett, award-winning author, lives on a farm in Georgia with her husband, two dogs, and chickens. She writes series for her readers: thriller, mystery, post-apocalyptic science fiction, and cozy mystery novels. Stories with a twist: not your typical characters from not your typical author!

Her motto: *You keep reading; I'll keep writing!*

When she isn't writing, Judith is working on farm chores, hiking or camping with her husband and dogs, or rocking on her front porch while she watches the sunset.

Website.     judithabarrett.com

VIP Readers  judithabarrett.com/newsletter

Facebook     Judith A. Barrett, Author

Exclusive Discounts and Sales  barrettbookshop.com

Not into emails, even though Judith's story-focused newsletters are interesting, Not-Your-Typical newsletters? Follow Judith on Barrett Book Shop, Her Blog on her website: The Latest Twist, Bookbub, or your favorite bookseller for news of her latest release!

www.ingramcontent.com/pod-product-compliance
Lightning Source LLC
Chambersburg PA
CBHW070220030726
47505CB00006B/1747